FRIDAY
THE RABBI
SLEPT LATE

HARRY KEMELMAN

FAWCETT CREST • NEW YORK

A Fawcett.Crest Book

Published by Ballantine Books

Copyright © 1964 by Harry Kemelman

ISBN 0-449-21180-0

This edition published by arrangement with Crown Publishers, Inc.

A Book-of-the-Month Club alternate selection

Manufactured in the United States of America

First Fawcett Crest Edition: November 1965
First Ballantine Books Edition: January 1984
Fourth Printing: December 1986

Fawcett Crest Books
by Harry Kemelman:

SUNDAY THE RABBI STAYED HOME
MONDAY THE RABBI TOOK OFF
TUESDAY THE RABBI SAW RED
WEDNESDAY THE RABBI GOT WET
THURSDAY THE RABBI WALKED OUT
FRIDAY THE RABBI SLEPT LATE
SATURDAY THE RABBI WENT HUNGRY
CONVERSATIONS WITH RABBI SMALL
SOMEDAY THE RABBI WILL LEAVE

**TO MY
FATHER AND MOTHER**

1

THEY SAT IN THE CHAPEL AND WAITED. THEY WERE STILL only nine, and they were waiting for the tenth so that they could begin morning prayers. The elderly president of the congregation, Jacob Wasserman, was wearing his phylacteries, and the young rabbi, David Small, who had just arrived, was putting his on. He had withdrawn his left arm from his jacket and rolled up his shirt sleeve to the armpit. Placing the little black box with its quotation from the Scriptures on the upper arm—next to the heart—he bound the attached strap seven times around his forearm, and then thrice around his palm to form the first letter of the Divine Name, and finally around his middle finger as a ring of spiritual betrothal to God. This, together with the headpiece which he now placed on his forehead, was in literal response to the biblical injunction: "Thou shalt bind them (the words of God) for a sign upon thine hand, and they shall be for a frontlet between thine eyes."

The others, who were dressed in silken-fringed prayer shawls and black skullcaps, sat around in small groups talking, glancing idly through their prayer books, occasionally checking their watches against the round clock on the wall.

1

The rabbi, now prepared for morning service, strolled up and down the center aisle, not impatiently, but like a man who has arrived early at the railroad station. Snatches of conversation reached him: talk about business, about family and children, about vacation plans, about the chances of the Red Sox. It was hardly the proper conversation for men waiting to pray, he thought, and then immediately rebuked himself. Was it not also a sin to be too devout? Was not man expected to enjoy the good things of this life? the pleasures of family? of work—and of resting from work? He was still very young, not quite thirty, and introspective, so that he could not help raising questions, and then questioning the questions.

Mr. Wasserman had left the room and now returned. "I just called Abe Reich. He said he'd be down in about ten minutes."

Ben Schwarz, a short, plumpish, middle-aged man, got up abruptly. "That does it for me," he muttered. "If I have to be beholden to that sonofabitch Reich to make up a minyan, I'll do my praying at home."

Wasserman hurried over and halted him at the end of the aisle. "Surely you're not going now, Ben? That will leave us only nine, even when Reich gets here."

"Sorry, Jacob," said Schwarz stiffly, "I've got an important appointment and I've got to leave."

Wasserman spread his hands. "You have come to say Kaddish for your father, so what kind of appointment can you have that can't wait a few minutes longer so you can pay respects to him?" In his mid-sixties, Wasserman was older than most of the members of the congregation, and he spoke with a faint accent which manifested itself not so much in mispronounced words as in the special care he took to pronounce them correctly. He saw that Schwarz was wavering. "Besides, I have Kaddish myself today, Ben."

"All right, Jacob, stop churning my emotions. I'll stay." He even grinned.

But Wasserman wasn't finished. "And why should you be sore at Abe Reich? I heard what you said. You two used to be such good friends."

Schwarz needed no prompting. "I'll tell you why. Last week—"

Wasserman held up his hand. "The business with the automobile? I heard it already. If you feel he owes you some money, sue him and get it over with."

"A case like this you don't take to court."

"Then settle your differences some other way. But in the temple we shouldn't have two prominent members who they can't even stand to be in the same minyan. It's a shame."

"Look, Jacob—"

"Did you ever think that's the real function of a temple in a community like his? It should be a place where Jews should settle their differences." He beckoned the rabbi over. "I was just saying to Ben here that the temple is a holy place, and all Jews who come here should be at peace with each other. Here they should make up their differences. Maybe that's more important for the temple than just a place to pray. What do you think?"

The young rabbi looked from one to the other uncertainly. He reddened. "I'm afraid I can't agree, Mr. Wasserman," he said. "The temple is not really a holy place. The original one was, of course, but a community synagogue like ours is just a building. It's for prayer and study, and I suppose it is holy in the sense that anywhere a group of men gathers to pray is holy. But settling differences is not traditionally the function of the temple, but of the rabbi."

Schwarz said nothing. He did not consider it good form for the young rabbi to contradict the president of the temple so openly. Wasserman was really his boss, besides being old enough to be his father. But Jacob did not seem to mind. His eyes twinkled and he even seemed pleased.

"So if two members of the temple quarrel, what would you suggest, rabbi?"

The young man smiled faintly. "Well, in the old days I would have suggested a Din Torah."

"What's that?" asked Schwarz.

"A hearing, a judgment," the rabbi answered. "That, incidentally, is one of the rabbi's main functions—to sit in judgment. In the old days, in the ghettos of Europe, the rabbi was hired not by the synagogue but by the town. And he was hired not to lead prayers or to supervise the synagogue, but to sit in judgment on cases that were brought to him, and to pass on questions of law."

"How did he make his decisions?" asked Schwarz, interested in spite of himself.

"Like any judge, he would hear the case, sometimes alone, sometimes in conjunction with a pair of learned men from the village. He would ask questions, examine witnesses if necessary, and then on the basis of the Talmud, he would give his verdict."

"I'm afraid that wouldn't help us much," said Schwarz with a smile. "This is about an automobile. I'm sure the Talmud doesn't deal with automobile cases."

"The Talmud deals with everything," said the rabbi flatly.

"But automobiles?"

"The Talmud doesn't mention automobiles, of course, but it does deal with such things as damages and responsibility. Particular situations differ from age to age, but the general principles remain the same."

"So, Ben," asked Wasserman, "are you ready to submit your case for judgment?"

"It wouldn't bother me any. I don't mind telling my story to anybody. The more the better. I'd just as soon the whole congregation knew what a louse Abe Reich is."

"No, I mean it seriously, Ben. You and Abe are both on the board of directors. You've both given I don't know how many hours of your time to the temple. Why not make use of the traditional Jewish way of settling an argument?"

Schwarz shrugged his shoulders. "As far as I'm concerned . . ."

"How about you, rabbi? Would you be willing—"

"If Mr. Reich and Mr. Schwarz are both willing, I will hold a Din Torah."

"You'll never get Abe Reich to come," Schwarz said.

"I'll guarantee that Reich will be there," said Wasserman.

Schwarz was interested now, even eager. "All right, how do we go about it? When do you have this—this Din Torah, and where do you have it?"

"Is this evening all right? In my study?"

"Fine with me, rabbi. You see, what happened was that Abe Reich—"

"If I am to hear the case," the rabbi asked gently, "don't you think you ought to wait until Mr. Reich is present before you tell your story?"

"Oh sure, rabbi. I didn't mean—"

"Tonight, Mr. Schwarz."

"I'll be there."

The rabbi nodded and strolled away. Schwarz watched his retreating figure and then said, "You know, Jacob, when you come right down to it, this is a kind of silly thing that I've agreed to do."

"Why silly?"

"Because—because here I've agreed to what amounts to a regular trial."

"So?"

"So who is the judge?" He nodded in the direction of the rabbi, moodily, noting the young man's ill-fitting suit, his rumpled hair, his dusty shoes. "Look at him—a boy, like a college kid. I'm practically old enough to be his father, and I should let him try me? You know, Jacob, if that's what a rabbi is supposed to be—I mean, a kind of judge—then maybe Al Becker and some of the others who say we ought to have an older, more mature man, maybe they're right. Do you really think Abe Reich will agree to all this?" A sudden thought occurred to him. "Say, Jacob, if Abe doesn't agree, I mean if he doesn't appear at the what-do-you-call-it, does that mean the case goes to me by default?"

"There's Reich now," said Wasserman. "We'll begin in a moment. And about tonight, don't worry; he'll be there."

The rabbi's study was on the second floor, overlooking the large asphalt parking lot. Mr. Wasserman arrived as the rabbi drove up, and the two men went upstairs together.

"I didn't know you were planning to come," said the rabbi.

"Schwarz began to get cold feet, so I said I would be present. Do you mind?"

5

"Not at all."

"Tell me, rabbi," Wasserman went on, "have you ever done this before?"

"Held a Din Torah? Of course not. As a Conservative rabbi, how would I have been likely to? For that matter, in Orthodox congregations here in America, who thinks to go to the rabbi for Din Torah these days?"

"But then—"

The rabbi smiled. "It will be all right, I assure you. I am not entirely unaware of what goes on in the community. I have heard rumors. The two men were always good friends and now something has come up to upset their friendship. My guess is that neither one is very happy about this quarrel and both are only too anxious to make up. Under the circumstances, I ought to be able to find some common ground between them."

"I see," said Wasserman, nodding. "I was beginning to be a little worried. As you say, they were friends. And that for a long time. In all probability when the story comes out it will turn out to be the wives that are behind it. Ben's wife, Myra, she's a regular *kochlefel*. She's got a tongue on her."

"I know," said the rabbi sadly. "Only too well."

"Schwarz is a weak man," Wasserman went on, "and in that household it's the wife who wears the pants. They used to be good neighbors, the Schwarzes and the Reichs, and then Ben Schwarz came into some money when his father died a couple of years ago. Come to think of it, it must have been a couple of years ago today, because he came to say Kaddish. They moved out to Grove Point and began to hobnob with the Beckers and the Pearlsteins—that crowd. I suspect that a good part of this is just Myra trying to break away from her old associations."

"Well, we'll know soon enough," said the rabbi. "That must be one of them now."

The front door banged and they heard steps on the stairs. The outer door opened and closed again and in came Ben Schwarz and, a moment later, Abe Reich. It was as though each had waited to see whether the other would show up. The rabbi motioned Schwarz to a seat at one side of the desk and Reich at the other.

6

Reich was a tall man, quite handsome, with a high forehead and iron-gray hair brushed back. There was a touch of the dandy about him. He wore a black suit with narrow lapels and side pockets aslant in the continental style. His trousers were slim and cuffless. He was the division sales manager of a national low-price shoe company and he had an air of dignity and executive decisiveness. He strove to hide his present embarrassment by looking indifferent.

Schwarz, too, was embarrassed, but he tried to pass off the whole matter as a joke, an elaborate gag his good friend Jake Wasserman had cooked up and which he was prepared to go along with, as a good guy.

Schwarz and Reich had not spoken since entering the room; in fact they avoided looking at each other. Reich began by talking to Wasserman, so Schwarz addressed himself to the rabbi.

"Well," he said with a grin, "what happens now? Do you put on your robe and do we all rise? Is Jacob the clerk of the court or is he the jury?"

The rabbi smiled. Then he hitched up his chair to indicate that he was ready to begin. "I think you both understand what's involved here," he said easily. "There are no formal rules of procedure. Normally it is customary for both sides to acknowledge the jurisdiction of the court and willingness to abide by the rabbi's decision. In this case I won't insist on it, however."

"I don't mind," said Reich. "I'm willing to abide by your decision."

Not to be outdone, Schwarz said, "I certainly don't have anything to fear. I'll go along, too."

"Fine," said the rabbi. "As the aggrieved party, Mr. Schwarz, I suggest that you tell us what happened."

"There isn't very much to tell," said Schwarz. "It's pretty simple. Abe, here, borrowed Myra's car, and through sheer negligence he ruined it. I'll have to pay for a whole new motor. That's it in a nutshell."

"Very few cases are that simple," said the rabbi. "Can you tell me the circumstances under which he took the car? And also, just to keep the record clear, is it your car or your wife's? You refer to it as your wife's, but then you say you will have to pay for the motor."

7

Schwarz smiled. "It's my car in the sense that I paid for it. And it's her car in the sense that it's the one she normally drives. It's a Ford convertible, a 'sixty-three. The car I drive is a Buick."

"Nineteen sixty-three?" The rabbi's eyebrows shot up. "Then it's practically a new car. Isn't it still within the guarantee period?"

"Are you kidding, rabbi?" Schwarz snorted. "No dealer considers himself bound if the damage is due to the owner's negligence. Becker Motors where I bought the car is as reliable as any dealer in the business, but Al Becker made me feel like a damn fool when I suggested it to him."

"I see," said the rabbi, and indicated that he should proceed.

"Well, there's a group of us who do things together—go on theater parties, auto trips, that sort of thing. It all started as a garden club made up of a few congenial couples who lived near each other, but some of us have moved out of the area. Still, we meet about once a month. This was a skiing party to Belknap in New Hampshire and we took two cars. The Alberts drove up with the Reichs in their sedan. I took the Ford and we had Sarah, Sarah Weinbaum, with us. She's a widow. The Weinbaums were part of the group, and since her husband died we try to include her in everything.

"We went up early Friday afternoon—it's only a three-hour ride—and were able to get some skiing in Friday before nightfall. We went out Saturday—all except Abe here. He had caught a bad cold and was sneezing and coughing. Then, Saturday night, Sarah got a call from her kids—she has two sons, one seventeen and one fifteen—to the effect that they had been in an automobile accident. They assured her it was nothing serious, and that's how it turned out—Bobby had got a scratch, and Myron, that's the oldest boy, had to have a couple of stitches. Still, Sarah was awfully upset and wanted to go home. Well, under the circumstances I couldn't blame her. Since she had come up with us, I offered to let her take our car. But it was late and foggy out, and Myra wouldn't hear of her going alone. So then Abe here volunteered to drive her back."

"Are you in agreement with what has been said so far, Mr. Reich?" asked the rabbi.

"Yes, that's what happened."

"All right, proceed, Mr. Schwarz."

"When we got home Sunday night, the car wasn't in the garage. That didn't disturb me, because obviously Abe wasn't going to leave it at our house and then walk to his. The next morning, I went off in my own car and my wife called him to make arrangements about delivering her car. And then he told her—"

"Just a minute, Mr. Schwarz. I take it that's as far as you can go with the story from your own knowledge. I mean, from here on you would be telling what your wife told you rather than what you yourself experienced."

"I thought you said we weren't going to have any legalistic rules—"

"We're not, but since we want to get the story down first, obviously it would be better to let Mr. Reich continue. I just want the story in chronological order."

"Oh, all right."

"Mr. Reich."

"It's just as Ben told it. I started out with Mrs. Weinbaum. It was foggy and dark of course, but we drove along at a good clip. Then, when we were getting home, the car slowed to a stop. Fortunately, a cruising car came along and the cop asked what the trouble was. I told him we couldn't get started, so he said he'd get us a tow. About five minutes later, a tow truck came from an outlying garage and pulled us to town. It was late then, past midnight I guess, and there was no mechanic in attendance. So I called a cab and took Mrs. Weinbaum home. And wouldn't you know it, when we got there the house was dark and Mrs. Weinbaum had forgotten her key."

"Then how did you get in?" asked the rabbi.

"She said she always left one of the windows unlatched and it could be reached by climbing the porch. The way I was feeling, I couldn't have made it up a steep flight of stairs, and of course she couldn't. The cabby was a young fellow but claimed he had a game leg. Maybe he did and maybe he didn't, and maybe he was afraid we were trying to get him involved in a burglary. But he did tell us that the night patrolman usually stopped for coffee and a cigarette at the milk plant about that time. By now Mrs. Weinbaum was almost frantic, so we sent the cabby after the cop, and just as they came back, who should drive up but the two boys. They'd gone to a movie in town! Well, I guess Mrs. Weinbaum was so relieved to see they were all right she didn't even bother to thank me, just swept into the house with them, leaving me to explain it to the cop.''

Schwarz, sensing an implied criticism, said, "Sarah must have been very upset because normally she's very considerate.''

Reich made no comment, but continued, "Well, I told the cop what had happened. He didn't say anything, just gave me that suspicious look they have. You can imagine how I felt by that time. My nose was stuffed up so I couldn't breathe, my bones ached, and I guess I was running a fever. I stayed in bed all day Sunday, and when my wife came home from Belknap, I was asleep and I didn't even hear her come in. The next morning, I still felt rotten so I decided not to go to the office. When Myra called, Betsy, my wife, answered. She woke me up and I told her what had happened and gave her the name of the garage, to give to Myra. Next thing I know, maybe ten minutes later, the phone rings again and it's Myra and she insists on talking to me. So I got out of bed and she tells me that she has just called the garage and they say that I ruined her car, that I ran it without oil and that the whole engine is junk and that she's holding me responsible, and so on and so forth. She was pretty rough over the phone, and I wasn't feeling too good, so I told her to do anything she darn pleased, and hung up on her and went back to bed.''

The rabbi looked questioningly at Schwarz.

"Well, according to my wife, he said some other things too, but I guess that's about what happened.''

The rabbi swiveled around in his chair and slid back the glass door of the bookcase behind him. He studied the books on the shelf for a moment, and then drew one out. Schwarz grinned, and catching Wasserman's eye, winked at him. Reich's mouth twitched as he suppressed a smile. The rabbi, however, was oblivious as he thumbed through the book. Every now and then, he halted at a page and skimmed through it, nodding his head. Occasionally, he massaged his forehead as if to stimulate cerebration. He looked about his desk nearsightedly and finally found a ruler, which he used to mark a place in the book. A moment later he used a paperweight to mark another. Then he drew out a second volume, and here he seemed more certain for he quickly found the passage he was looking for. Finally he pushed both volumes away and looked benignly at the two men before him.

"There are certain aspects of the case that are not entirely clear to me. I notice, for example, that you, Mr. Schwarz, speak of Sarah, whereas you, Mr. Reich, speak of Mrs. Weinbaum. Does this indicate merely a greater informality in Mr. Schwarz, or that the lady is closer to the Schwarzes than she is to the Reichs?"

"She was a member of the group. We were all friends. If any one of us had a party or an affair, they would invite her just as we did."

The rabbi looked at Reich, who said, "I'd say she was closer to them. We met the Weinbaums through Ben and Myra. They were particularly friendly."

"Yes, perhaps that's so," Schwarz admitted. "What of it?"

"And it was in your car that she drove up to the skiing area?" asked the rabbi.

"Yes, although it just worked out that way. What are you driving at?"

"I am suggesting that she was essentially your guest, and that you felt a greater sense of responsibility for her than did Mr. Reich."

Mr. Wasserman leaned forward.

"Yes, I suppose that's so," Schwarz admitted again.

"Then in driving her home, wasn't Mr. Reich in a sense doing you a favor?"

"He was doing himself a favor too. He had a bad cold and wanted to get home."

"Had he made any suggestions to that effect before Mrs. Weinbaum received the call?"

"No, but we all knew he wanted to get home."

"If the call had not come, do you think he would have asked for your car?"

"Probably not."

"Then I think we may leave it that in driving Mrs. Weinbaum home he was doing you a favor, however advantageous it may have been to himself."

"Well, I don't see that it makes any difference. What of it?"

"Just this, that in the one case he would be in the position of a borrower, but in the second case he is in effect your agent, and a different set of rules applies. As a borrower, the responsibility of returning your car in good condition rests squarely on him, and to avoid liability he would have to prove that there was a flaw in the car and also that there was no negligence on his part. Furthermore, it would be his responsibility to make sure that the car was in good condition when he took it. As an agent, on the other hand, he has a right to assume that the car was in good condition and the burden of proof rests with you. It is you who has to prove that he was grossly negligent."

Wasserman smiled.

"I don't see that it makes much difference. I feel that in either case he was grossly negligent. And I can prove it. There wasn't a drop of oil in the car. That's what the garage mechanic said. Now, he let the oil run dry and that is gross negligence."

"How would I know the oil was low?" demanded Reich.

Until now, both men had addressed themselves to the rabbi, talking to each other through him. But now Schwarz swung around and facing Reich directly, said, 'You stopped for gas, didn't you?"

Reich also turned in his chair. "Yes, I stopped for gas. When I got into the car I noticed you had less than half a tank, so after we'd been driving for about an hour, I pulled into a station and told him to fill her up."

"But you didn't tell him to check the oil," said Schwarz.

"No, and I didn't tell him to check the water in the radiator or in the battery or the pressure in the tires. I had a nervous, hysterical woman on the seat beside me who could hardly wait until he finished pumping the gas. Why did I have to check everything out? It was practically a new car. It wasn't a jalopy.''

"And yet Sarah told Myra that she mentioned the oil to you.''

"Sure, after we had driven on about five or ten miles. I asked her why should I, and she said you had on the way up and that you had put in a couple of quarts. So I said, Then certainly we don't need any, and that ended that. She dozed off and didn't wake up until we got stalled and she thought we were home.''

"Well, I would say it's customary when taking a long trip to check oil and water every time you stop,'' insisted Schwarz.

"Just a minute, Mr. Schwarz,'' said the rabbi, "I am no mechanic, but I don't understand why a new car would need a couple of quarts of oil.''

"Because there was a small leak in the seal, but it was nothing serious. I noticed a few drops of oil on the garage floor and spoke to Al Becker about it. He said he'd take care of it but that I could drive all right until I got around to bringing it in.''

The rabbi looked at Reich to see if he had anything to say in reply, and then leaned back in his swivel chair and considered. Finally, he straightened up with a jerk of his shoulders. He patted the books on the desk. "These are two of the three volumes of the Talmud that deal with the general subject of what we would call torts. The subject is treated very fully. This first volume treats of the general causes of damages, and the section that concerns an ox that gores, for example, goes on for about forty pages. A general principle is evolved which the rabbis applied broadly to all kinds of cases. It is the basic distinction they made between *tam* and *muad*, that is, between the docile ox and the ox that has already earned a reputation as a vicious beast by virtue of having gored on several occasions in the past. The owner of the latter was felt to be far more responsible in the event of a goring than the former, since he already had had warning and should have taken special precautions.'' He glanced at Mr. Wasserman, who nodded in corroboration.

The rabbi got up from behind his desk and began to

pace the floor. His tone took on the singsong quality traditional with Talmudists as he followed the thread of the argument. "Now in this case, you knew your car leaked oil. And I suggest, that, at least while it was being driven, it leaked more than just a few drops, since you found it necessary to add two full quarts on the trip up. If Mr. Reich had been a borrower—and we come now to this volume which deals with the subject of borrowing as well as the law of agency—if Mr. Reich, for example, had said that he did not feel well and wanted to go home and had asked to borrow your car for the trip, it would have been his responsibility either to ask you if it were in good condition, or himself to check it. And if he failed to do so, even if the circumstances had been precisely the same as they were, then he would have been responsible and liable for the damage done. But we have already agreed that he was not a borrower but essentially your agent, and hence the responsibility was yours to inform him that the car leaked oil and to watch and see that it did not drop below the safe level."

"Just a minute, rabbi," said Schwarz. "I didn't have to warn him personally. The car has a built-in warning device—the oil light. When a man drives a car, he's supposed to watch his instruments, and if he had, the red light would have told him he was getting dangerously low."

The rabbi nodded. "That is a good point. Mr. Reich?"

"As a matter of fact, the light did go on," he said. "But when it did we were on the open road without a station in sight, and before I could find one we'd stalled."

"I see," said the rabbi.

"But according to the mechanic, he should have smelled something burning long before," Schwarz insisted.

"Not if his nose was stuffed up with a bad cold. And Mrs. Weinbaum, you remember, was asleep." The rabbi shook his head. "No, Mr. Schwarz, Mr. Reich did only what the average driver would have done under the existing road conditions. Therefore, he could not be considered negligent, and if not negligent, then not responsible."

The finality in his tone indicated that the hearing was

over. Reich was the first to rise. "This has been a revelation to me, rabbi," he said in a low voice. The rabbi acknowledged his thanks.

Reich turned uncertainly to Schwarz, hoping he would make some gesture of reconciliation, but he remained seated, his eyes focused on the floor as he rubbed the palms of his hands together in vexation.

Reich waited an awkward moment, then said, "Well, I'll be going." At the door he paused. "I didn't see your car in the parking lot, Jacob. Can I give you a lift?"

"Yes, I walked," said Wasserman, "but I think I'd like a ride home."

"I'll wait downstairs."

Only when the door closed did Schwarz raise his head. It was obvious he was hurt. "I guess I had the wrong idea of what this hearing was supposed to do, rabbi. Or maybe you had the wrong idea. I told you, or I tried to tell you, that I wasn't planning to bring suit against Abe. After all, I could afford the repairs a lot better than he could. If he had come forward with an offer of some kind I would have refused it, but we would have remained friends. Instead, he was nasty to my wife, and a man has to back up his wife. I suppose she gave him the rough side of her tongue. And I can understand now why he reacted the way he did."

"Well then—"

Schwarz shook his head. "You don't understand, rabbi. I was hoping that this hearing would effect some kind of compromise, that it would sort of bring us together. Instead, you cleared him completely, which means that I must have been entirely in the wrong. But I don't feel I was all wrong. After all, what did I do? A couple of friends of mine wanted to get home in a hurry and I lent them my car. Was that wrong? It seems to me that you were not acting as an impartial judge, but more like his lawyer. All your questions and your arguments were directed towards me. I don't have the legal training to see the flaw in your line of reasoning, but I'm sure that if I had counsel here to represent me, he would. In any case, I'm sure he would have been able to work out some sort of compromise."

"But we did even better than that," said the rabbi.

15

"How do you mean? You cleared him of negligence and I'm going to be several hundred dollars out of pocket."

The rabbi smiled. "I'm afraid that you do not grasp the full significance of the evidence, Mr. Schwarz. True, Mr. Reich was cleared of all negligence, but that doesn't automatically make you culpable."

"I don't get it."

"Let us consider what we have here. You bought a car with a leaking seal. And when you noticed the damage, you notified the manufacturer through his representative, Mr. Becker. Now, it is true that the fault was a minor one and that neither Mr. Becker nor you had reason to believe it might become more serious in the immediate future. The likelihood that it might become aggravated by a long trip evidently did not occur to him, else he would have warned you against it, in which case I'm sure you would not have used that car to go up to New Hampshire. But the fact is that driving for a long distance at a high rate of speed did result in expanding the leak, which is why you had to put in a couple of quarts of oil on the way up. Now, under these circumstances, the manufacturer can only require of you that you use normal caution. I think you will agree that Mr. Reich did nothing any cautious driver would not have—"

"So it was really their fault, rabbi?" Schwarz's face showed animation and there was excitement in his voice. "Is that what you're saying?"

Mr. Wasserman smiled broadly.

"Precisely, Mr. Schwarz. It is my contention that it was the fault of the manufacturer and that he must make good under his warranty."

"Well gee, rabbi, that's swell. I'm sure Becker will come across. After all, it's no skin off his nose. Then that makes everything all right. Look, rabbi, if I said anything that—"

The rabbi cut him off. "Quite understandable under the circumstances, Mr. Schwarz."

Schwarz was for taking everyone out for a drink, but the rabbi excused himself. "If you don't mind, some other night perhaps. As I was leafing through those books, I came across a couple of points that interested me. Nothing to do with all this, but I'd like to check them over while they're fresh in my mind." He shook hands with the two men and took them to the door.

"Well, what do you think of the rabbi now?" Wasserman could not help asking on the way downstairs.

"He's quite a guy," said Schwarz.

"A gaon, Ben, a regular gaon."

"I don't know what a gaon is, Jacob, but if you say so, I'll take your word for it."

"And what about Abe?"

"Well, Jacob, between me and you, it was mostly Myra. You know how women are about losing a few bucks."

From the window of his study, the rabbi looked down at the parking lot below to see the three men talking in obvious reconciliation. He smiled and turned from the window. The books on his desk caught his eye. Adjusting the reading lamp, he sat down behind the desk and pulled the books toward him.

2

ELSPETH BLEECH LAY ON HER BACK AND WATCHED THE CEILing slowly tilt, first to one side and then the other. She clutched at the bedclothes as though afraid she might fall out of bed. The alarm clock had awakened her as usual, but as she sat up the vertigo struck and she let her head fall back on the pillow.

The sun slanting in through the slats of the venetian blind gave promise of a perfect June day. She shut her eyes tight to blot out the moving walls and ceiling, but she could sense the sun in a sort of red haze, and at the same time she felt as though the bed were rocking sickeningly under her. Although the morning was cool, her forehead was wet with perspiration.

By an effort of will she sat up again, and then without bothering to put on her slippers fled to the tiny bathroom. After a while she felt better, and came back and sat on the edge of the bed and dried her face, wondering dully if she ought not lie down for another half-hour or so. As if in answer there came a pound on the door and the children, Angelina and Johnnie, shouted, "Elspeth, Elspeth, dress us. We want to go out."

"All right, Angie," she called back. "You and Johnnie go back upstairs and play quietly, and Elspeth will be up in a minute. Now remember, play quietly. You don't want to wake your mummy and daddy."

Fortunately they obeyed, and she sighed with relief. Slipping on a robe and slippers, she brewed herself a cup of tea and made some toast. The food made her feel better.

She had been having strange symptoms for a while, but lately they had grown worse. Today was the second day in a row she had been sick. When it happened yesterday morning, she had assumed it was the ravioli Mrs. Serafino had given her for supper the night before; maybe she had eaten more than was good for her. But yesterday she had eaten sparingly—all day—perhaps she had not eaten enough.

She might even speak to her friend Celia Saunders. Celia was older and should know something she could take for it. At the same time, she realized it would be unwise to detail the symptoms too precisely. In the back of her mind was the fear that possibly, just possibly, her sickness might be due to something quite different.

The children in the room overhead were getting noisy. She did not want Mrs. Serafino to see her until she was fully dressed and had had a chance to put a touch of color on her cheeks. She was even more anxious lest Mr. Serafino see her that way, and she hurried back to her room to dress. Taking off her robe and nightgown, she surveyed herself in the full-length mirror on the closet door. She was sure she did not look any stouter. Nevertheless, she decided to put on the new girdle that was firmer than her old one and held her in better.

By the time she was dressed, she felt her old self again. Just the sight of herself in the mirror, trim in her white uniform, made her spirits rise. Suppose it was the other thing? It need not necessarily be dreaded; she might even use it to advantage. But of course she'd have to be sure, and that meant a trip to the doctor, perhaps this Thursday on her day off.

"Then why the hell don't you get the rabbi to write the letter to the Ford Company?" demanded Al Becker. He was a short, stocky man with a powerful torso mounted on short, stumpy legs. Nose and chin both protruded combatively and there was a pugnacious twist to his lipless mouth, out of which jutted a thick, black cigar. When he removed it from the corner of his mouth, he held it between the curled first and second fingers of his right hand, so that it seemed like a glowing weapon in a clenched fist. His eyes were dull blue marbles.

Ben Schwarz had come to him full of glad tidings. He thought his good friend would be happy to hear he wouldn't have to stand the considerable expense of mounting a new motor in the car.

But Becker had been far from pleased. True, it would cost Becker Motors nothing, but it did mean a lot of trouble, perhaps extensive correspondence to explain the matter to the company.

"How does the rabbi get into things like this?" he wanted to know. "You're a sensible feller, Ben. Now I ask you, is this the function of a rabbi of a temple?"

"But you don't understand, Al," Schwarz said. "It wasn't the question of repairs on the car at all. It was, of course, but—"

"Well, was it or wasn't it?"

"Well, sure it was, but I mean I didn't go to him about that. He happened to hear I was sore at Abe Reich so he suggested a Din Torah—"

"A Din who?"

"Din Torah," said Schwarz carefully. "It's when two parties to a conflict or an argument go to the rabbi and he hears the case and makes a judgment according to the Talmud. It's a regular thing that rabbis do."

"First I heard of it."

"Well, I admit I didn't know about it before myself. Anyway, I agreed, and Reich and I and Wasserman—as a kind of witness, I suppose—went to the rabbi, and he worked the whole thing out so that it was plain that neither Reich nor I had been negligent. And by God, if I wasn't negligent and the driver of the car wasn't negligent, then the fault was in the car and the company is supposed to make good."

"Well, goddammit, the company won't make good unless I say so, and I can just see myself going to them for a job this big with that kind of cock-and-bull story."

Becker's voice was never soft, and when he was angry he shouted.

Schwarz seemed suddenly deflated. "But there was a leak in the seal," he shouted back. "I told you about that."

"Sure, a couple of drops a week. That kind of leak wouldn't burn out a motor."

"A couple of drops when she was standing still. But she must have been gushing when I drove. I put two quarts in on my way to New Hampshire. That's no couple of drops. Now that I know from my own knowledge."

The door of Becker's office opened and his junior partner, Melvin Bronstein, came in. Bronstein was a youngish man of forty, tall and slim with wavy black hair just beginning to gray at the temples; deep, dark eyes, an aquiline nose, and sensitive lips.

"What's going on?" he asked. "Is it a private argument, or can anyone join? I'll bet they could hear you guys down the block."

"What's going on is that in our temple we've got ourselves a rabbi who can be depended on to do everything except what he's supposed to do," said Becker.

Bronstein looked at Schwarz for enlightenment. Happy to have a somewhat less overpowering audience, Schwarz told his story while Becker rustled papers on his desk in elaborate unconcern.

Bronstein beckoned from the doorway of the office, and somewhat reluctantly Becker went over. Schwarz turned away so he would not appear to eavesdrop.

"Ben is a good customer of ours, Al," whispered Bronstein. "I don't think the company would question it."

"Yeah? Well, I've had dealings with the Ford Company since before you got out of high school, Mel," said Becker aloud.

But Bronstein knew his partner. He grinned at him. "Look, Al, if you turn Ben down you'll only have Myra to deal with. Isn't she president of the temple Sisterhood this year?"

"And last year, too," Ben could not help adding.

"It won't do our business any good to have her sore at us," Bronstein said, once again lowering his voice.

"Well, the Sisterhood don't buy cars."

"But the husbands of all the members do."

"Goddammit, Mel, how am I going to explain that I want the company to put a new engine in a car because the rabbi of my temple decided they ought to?"

"You don't have to mention the rabbi at all. You don't even have to explain how it happened. You can just say that the seal let go while the car was being driven."

"And what if the company sends down an investigator?"

"Have they ever done it to you, Al?"

"No, but they have with some other agencies."

"All right," said Bronstein with a grin, "if he comes, you can introduce him to your rabbi."

Suddenly Becker's mood changed. He chuckled deep in his throat and turned to Schwarz. "All right, Ben, I'll write the company and see if they'll go along. I'm only doing it, you understand, because you sold Mel here a bill of goods. He's the original big-hearted kid, the softest touch in town."

"Aw, you're just teed off because the rabbi was involved," said Bronstein. He turned to Schwarz. "Al would have gone along from the beginning, and glad of a chance to help out a customer, too, if you hadn't mentioned the rabbi."

"What have you got against the rabbi, Al?" asked Ben.

"What have I got against the rabbi?" Becker removed the cigar from his mouth. "I'll tell you what I've got against the rabbi. He's not the man for the job; that's what I've got against him. He's supposed to be our representative, yet would you hire him as a salesman for your company, Ben? Come on now, be truthful."

"Sure, I'd hire him," said Schwarz, but his tone did not carry conviction.

"Well, if you were fool enough to hire him, I hope you would be smart enough to fire him the first time he got out of line."

"When has he got out of line?" demanded Schwarz.

"Oh, come on, Ben. How about the time we had the Fathers and Sons breakfast and we brought down Barney Gilligan of the Red Sox to talk to the kids. He gets up to introduce him and what does he say? He gives the kids a long spiel about how our heroes are scholars instead of athletes. I could've gone through the floor."

"Well . . ."

"And how about the time your own wife had him come down to pep up the girls of the Sisterhood to put on a big campaign for a Chanukah gift for the temple, and he tells them that keeping Judaism in their hearts and a kosher home was more important for Jewish women than campaigning for gifts for the temple."

"Just a minute, Al. Naturally I wouldn't say anything against my own wife, but right is right. That was a luncheon meeting, and Myra served shrimp cocktail, which ain't kosher-type food and which you couldn't blame a rabbi for being sore about."

"And with all this in-fighting going on, you keep trying to get me to join the temple," said Bronstein with a wink at Schwarz.

"Sure," said his partner, "because as a Jew and a resident of Barnard's Crossing you owe it to yourself and to your community to become a member. As for the rabbi, he won't be there forever, you know."

3

THE BOARD OF DIRECTORS WERE USING ONE OF THE EMPTY classroom to hold their regular Sunday meeting. Jacob Wasserman, as the president of the temple and chairman of the board, sat at the teacher's desk. The rest, fifteen of them, had squeezed themselves into the pupils' seats, their legs stretched out uncomfortably in the aisles. A few in back were sitting on the desks themselves, their feet on the chairs in front. Except for Wasserman, the board was composed of younger men, half still in their thirties and the rest in their forties and early fifties. Wasserman was dressed in a lightweight business suit, but the others wore the conventional costume in Barnard's Crossing for a warm Sunday in June—slacks, sport shirts, and jackets or golf sweaters.

Through the open windows came the roar of a power lawn mower operated by Stanley, the janitor. Through the open door came the shrill chanting of the children in the assembly down the hall. There was little formality to the proceedings, members speaking whenever they felt like it, and more often than not, as now, several at once.

The chairman rapped on the desk with a ruler. "Gentlemen, one at a time. Now what were you saying, Joe?"

"What I was *trying* to say is that I don't see how we

24

can transact business in all this noise. And I don't see why we don't use the small sanctuary for our regular meetings."

"Out of order," called another voice. "That's Good and Welfare."

"Why am I out of order?" demanded Joe belligerently. "All right, I'll make a motion that all meetings be conducted in the small sanctuary from now on. That's New Business."

"Gentlemen, gentlemen. As long as I'm chairman, anyone who has something important to say can say it any time. Our meetings aren't so complicated that we can't go out of order occasionally. The secretary can always set it right in his minutes. The only reason we aren't using the sanctuary, Joe, is that there's no place for the secretary to write on. However, if the members feel that a classroom like this is not a good place for a meeting, we could have Stanley set up a table in the sanctuary."

"That brings up another point, Jacob. How about Stanley? I don't think it looks right to our Gentile neighbors for him to be out working in plain sight on Sunday, especially since he's a Gentile and it's his holiday as much as theirs."

"What do you suppose they do on a Sunday? You walk along Vine Street and you'll see practically every one of them out cutting the lawn, trimming the hedge, or maybe painting their boat."

"Still, Joe has a good point there," said Wasserman. "Of course, if Stanley objected we certainly wouldn't insist. He's got to work here Sundays because of the school, but maybe it would be better if he kept inside. On the other hand, nobody tells him to work outside. In that respect, he's his own boss. He can arrange his work any way he wants. He's outside now because he wants to be."

"Yeah, but it doesn't look right."

"Well, it's only for a couple more weeks," said Wasserman. "During the summer, he has Sundays off." He hesitated and glanced at the clock at the back of the room. "That brings up a matter I'd like to talk about for a minute. We've got a couple of more meetings before

25

we adjourn for the summer, but I think we ought to consider the rabbi's contract."

"What about it, Jacob? It runs through the High Holidays, doesn't it?"

"That's true, it does. That's the way rabbis' contracts are always written, so that the temple always has a rabbi for the holiday services. Which is why it's customary to consider the new contract at this time of year. Then if the congregation decides they want to make a change, they have a chance to look around for a new rabbi. And if the rabbi wants to make a change, it gives him a chance to line up a new congregation. I think it might be a good idea if we voted right now to extend our rabbi's contract for another year, and send him a letter to that effect."

"Why? Is he looking around for something else, or did he mention it to you?"

Wasserman shook his head. "No, he hasn't spoken about it. I just think it might be a good idea to send him a letter before he does."

"Just a minute, Jacob, how do we know the rabbi wants to continue? Hadn't we ought to get a letter from him first?"

"I think he likes it here and I think he'd be willing to continue," said Wasserman. "As for the letter, it's usually the employer who notifies. Naturally, we'd have to give him a raise. I think an increase of five hundred dollars would be a proper token of appreciation."

"Mr. Chairman." It was the harsh voice of Al Becker. The vice-president straddled his chair and leaned forward, supporting his heavy torso on clenched fists on the desk in front of him. "Mr. Chairman, it seems to me that with the tough time we're having, with a brand-new temple and all, that five hundred dollars is a pretty expensive token."

"Yeah, five hundred dollars is a lot of money."

"He's only been here a year."

"Well, that's the best time to give it to him, isn't it, right after his first year?"

"You've got to give him some kind of a raise, and five hundred dollars is only a little more than five percent of his salary."

"Gentlemen, gentlemen." Wasserman rapped on the desk with the ruler.

"I move we lay the whole matter on the table for a week or two," said Meyer Goldfarb.

"What's to lay on the table?"

"Meyer always wants to postpone when it comes to spending money."

"It only hurts for a little while."

"Mr. Chairman." It was Al Becker again. "I second Meyer's motion to lay the matter on the table until next week. That's been our rule—whenever something involved spending a lot of money we've always held it over for at least a week. Now, I consider this a large expenditure. Five hundred dollars is a lot of money, and the new salary, ten thousand dollars, is an awful lot of money. All we've got here now is a bare quorum. I think on a matter as important as this, we ought to have a larger turnout. I move that Lennie be instructed to write to all members of the board asking them to be sure to come to next week's meeting to discuss a matter of special importance."

"There's a motion on the floor."

"Well, it's the same idea. All right, I'll make mine an amendment to the motion."

"Any discussion on the amendment?" asked Wasserman.

"Just a minute, Mr. Chairman," called Meyer Goldfarb. "That amendment is to my motion, so if I accept it then we don't have to have any discussion. I just change my motion, see."

"All right, restate your motion then."

"I move that the motion to extend the rabbi's contract—"

"Just a minute, Meyer, there was no such motion."

"Jacob made the motion."

"Jacob didn't make any motion. He just made a suggestion. Besides, he was in the chair—"

"Gentlemen," said Wasserman, banging with his ruler, "what's the sense of all this motion, amendment, amendment to the amendment. I didn't make a motion, I did make a motion? Is it the sense of this meeting that we

27

should put off any action on the rabbi's contract until next week?"

"Yeah."

"Sure, why not? The rabbi won't run away."

"Even out of respect to the rabbi, there ought to be more people here."

"All right," said Wasserman, "so let's hold it over already. If there's no other business"—he waited for a moment—"then this meeting stands adjourned."

4

Tuesday the weather was fine and mild, and Elspeth Bleech and her friend Celia Saunders, who took care of the Hoskins' children a couple of doors away, led their charges to the park, a ragged bit of turf a few blocks beyond the temple. The little procession was essentially a herding operation. The children ran ahead, but because Johnnie Serafino was still very young, Elspeth always took the stroller along. Sometimes he walked with the two women, his little fist tightly clutching the side or the chrome handle of the carriage, and sometimes he would clamber aboard and insist on being pushed.

Elspeth and Celia would walk about fifty feet and then stop to check on the whereabouts of their charges. If they had fallen behind they called to them, or ran back to pull them apart or make them drop something they had found in the gutter or a trash barrel.

Celia tried to persuade her friend to spend Thursday, their day off, together in Salem. "They're having a sale at Adelson's, and I wanted to see about another bathing suit. We could take the one o'clock bus—"

"I was thinking of going to Lynn," said Elspeth.

"Why Lynn?"

"Well, I've been feeling sort of, you know, sickly

29

lately and I thought I ought to have a check-up by a doctor. Maybe he could give me a tonic, or something."

"You don't need no tonic, El. What you need is a little exercise and some relaxation. Now you take my advice. You come into Salem with me and we can do some shopping, and then we can take in a movie in the afternoon. We can have a bite somewhere and after that we can go bowling. There's the nicest bunch of fellows come down the alleys Thursday nights. We have the grandest times just kidding around. No rough stuff and nobody gets fresh. We just have a lot of fun hacking around."

"Hm—I guess it's nice all right, but I just don't feel up to it, Cele. I'm tired most afternoons, and in the mornings I wake up and I feel light-headed, kind of."

"Well, I know the reason for that," said Celia positively.

"You do?"

"You just don't get enough sleep. That's your trouble. Staying up until two or three o'clock every morning, it's a wonder to me you can stand on your feet. And six days a week. I don't know of another girl who doesn't get Sundays off. Them Serafinos are taking advantage of you—they're working you to death."

"Oh, I get enough sleep. I don't have to stay up until they get home." She shrugged. "It's just that alone in the house with only the kids, I kind of don't like to get undressed and into bed. Most of the time, I nap on the couch. And then I nap in the afternoon, too. I get plenty of sleep, Cele."

"But Sundays—"

"Well, it's the only day they have for visiting their friends. I don't mind really. And Mrs. Serafino told me when I first came that anytime I wanted a Sunday off she would arrange for it. They're really quite nice to me. Mr. Serafino said that if I wanted to go downtown to church, he'd drive me—the buses being so bad on Sundays."

Celia halted in her stride and looked at Elspeth. "Tell me, does he ever bother you any?"

"Bother me?"

"You know, does he ever try to get fresh when the missus isn't around?"

"Oh no," said Elspeth quickly. "Where'd you get that idea?"

"I don't trust those nightclub types. And I don't like the way he looks at a girl."

"That's silly. He hardly says two words to me."

"Is it? Well, let me tell you something—Gladys, that's the girl that had your job before you—Mrs. Serafino fired her because she caught her husband fooling around with her. And she didn't have half your looks."

Stanley Doble was a typical Barnard's Crosser. Of a certain segment of Old Town society, he might even be considered the prototype. He was a thick-set man of forty, with sandy, graying hair. His deeply tanned, leathery skin indicated that he spent most of his time outdoors. He could build a boat. He could repair and install the plumbing and electric wiring in a house. He could take care of a lawn, trimming and mowing and raking tirelessly in the hot summer sun. He could repair an automobile, or the engine of a launch as it rose and fell in a heavy sea. At one time or another, he had earned his living doing each of these as well as by fishing and lobstering. At no time did he ever have trouble getting some kind of work; and at no time did he ever work long enough to make much more than he needed, until he came to work for the temple. This job he had held ever since they first acquired an old mansion and renovated it to serve as a combination school, community center, and synagogue. He had been all-important then, for without him the building would have fallen apart. He kept the boiler running, he fixed the plumbing and the wiring, he repaired the roof, and he spent the summer in painting the building inside and out. Since the completion of the new temple, his work had changed, of course. There was little repair work, but he kept the building clean and the lawn trimmed, regulated the heating system in the winter and the air conditioner when it got warm.

And now, on this bright Tuesday morning, he was raking up the temple lawn. He had already gathered several bushel baskets of lawn clippings and leaves.

Although there was the other side to do yet, as much again and more, he decided to stop for lunch. Then after lunch, if he felt like it, he could tackle the other side or let it go until the next day. There was no real hurry.

He had a bottle of milk and some sliced cheese in the refrigerator in the kitchen. Certain meats, actually any meats except those bought in particular stores—what he called 7WD stores, which was the way he read כשר‏, the Hebrew sign for kosher—he wasn't supposed to put in there. But milk and cheese were all right since they involved no slaughter and were ritually clean. Then he wondered if he wouldn't rather have a glass of beer. His car, a disreputable 1947 Ford convertible with no top and painted bright yellow from the remains of his last house-painting job, was in the parking lot in front of the temple. He could drive to the Ship's Cabin and still be back inside of an hour. There was no one he had to report to, but Mrs. Schwarz had said something about perhaps needing him to help decorate the vestry for the Sisterhood meeting, so he thought he had better be around. Besides, if he got involved in one of the interminable arguments in the Ship's Cabin, like whether shingle or clapboard was better for a house that faced the sea, or whether the Celtics would win the championship, there was no telling when he would get back.

He washed up, got his milk and cheese out of the refrigerator and brought them down to his own private corner in the basement where he had a rickety table, a cot, and a wicker armchair that he had retrieved from the town dump on one of his many excursions there, a favorite pastime of some segments of Barnard's Crossing society. He sat at the table and munched the sandwiches he had made, taking deep swallows from the mouth of the milk carton and staring moodily out of the narrow cellar window, watching the legs of passers-by through the bushes, men's legs encased in trousers, and silk-stockinged women's legs, slim and cool. Sometimes he would lean to one side, the better to follow an exceptional pair of women's legs until they passed the basement window. He would nod his grizzled head approvingly and breathe, "Beauty?"

He finished the quart of milk and wiped his mouth with the back of a gnarled, hairy hand. Rising from his chair, he stretched lazily, and then sat down again, on the cot this time, and scratched his rib-cage and his grizzled head with strong, stubby fingers. He lay back, wriggling his head against the pillow to form a comfortable hollow. For a moment he stared straight up at the pipes and conductors that ran across the ceiling like veins and arteries in an anatomy chart. Then his eyes wandered to the wall where he had pasted up a gallery of "art photos," pictures of women in various stages of undress. They were all buxom and saucy and inviting, and as his eyes roamed from one to another, his mouth relaxed in a smile of contentment.

From outside, just in front of his window, came the sound of women's voices. He rolled over to see who was talking and made out two pairs of women's legs, both encased in white stockings, and just beyond, the wheels of a stroller or baby carriage. He thought he knew who they were, having seen them pass often enough. It gave him special pleasure to eavesdrop on their conversation, almost as though he were peeping at them through a keyhole.

". . . then when you're through, you could take the bus to Salem and I could meet you and we could eat at the station."

"I kind of thought I'd stay on in Lynn and go to the Elysium."

"But they've got that picture that takes forever. How will you get home?"

"I checked, and it gets out at eleven-thirty. That will give me enough time to make the last bus."

"Aren't you afraid to go home alone that late at night?"

"Oh, there are plenty of people on that bus, and it's only a couple of blocks beyond the bus stop—Angie, you come right here this minute."

There was a scurry of a child's feet and then the women's legs marched out of view.

He rolled over on his back again and studied the pictures on the wall. One was of a dark girl who was naked except for a narrow garter belt and a pair of black stockings. As he concentrated on the picture, her hair became blonde and her stockings white. Presently his mouth dropped open and he began to snore, a steady, rhythmic, guttural throb like a boat engine in a heavy sea.

Myra Schwarz and the two women of the Sisterhood who were decorating the vestry for the box-supper meeting stood back, their heads tilted to one side.

"Can you get it just a little higher, Stanley?" asked Myra. "What do you think, girls?"

Stanley, perched on a stepladder, obediently raised the crepe paper a couple of inches.

"I think it should be a little lower down."

"Perhaps you're right. Can you lower it a hair, Stanley?"

He dropped it to where it had been before.

"Hold it right there, Stanley," called Myra. "That's just right, isn't it, girls?"

Enthusiastically they agreed. They were very much her junior in the organization; Emmy Adler was barely thirty, and Nancy Drettman, though older, had joined the Sisterhood only recently. As the decorating committee, they had come to the temple in slacks, prepared to work, when Myra, all dressed up, dropped in "to see if everything was going all right" and took over. They had no great passion for decorating, but it was one of those jobs given to newer members. Once they had demonstrated their willingness to work, more important jobs would be assigned to them—such as the advertising committee, which required them to badger the local tradespeople and their husbands' business associates for ads for the Program Book; the friendship committee, where they would visit the sick; and finally, having shown they could get things done, which usually meant coaxing other people to do them, they would see their names on the slate of candidates for positions on the executive council—and they would have arrived.

In the meantime, they practiced by ordering Stanley around. When they had first appeared, fully an hour before Mrs. Schwarz, they asked his help even though they knew he would much rather be outside working on the lawn. "Why don't you two ladies go on ahead and get started," he'd said. "I'll come along in a little while."

Mrs. Schwarz, on the other hand, had brooked no nonsense. She had said decisively, "Stanley, I need your help."

"I got this raking to do, Mrs. Schwarz," he had said.

"That can wait."

"Yes'm, I'll be right there," and put aside his rake and went to fetch the ladder.

It was a tiresome, tedious job, and he took no pleasure in it. Nor did he like working under the supervision of women—hard, brassy women like Mrs. Schwarz. He had just finished tacking the decoration in place when the door opened and the rabbi thrust his head in. "Oh, Stanley," he called out, "could I talk to you for a minute?"

Stanley promptly came down from the ladder, causing the crepe paper decoration to sag. The tack pulled out of the wall and there was a collective groan from the three women. The rabbi, aware of them for the first time, nodded half-apologetically for intruding and then turned to Stanley. "I'm expecting some books to be delivered by express," he said. "They should be here in a day or two. They're rare and quite valuable, so when they arrive please put them right in my study. Don't leave them lying around."

"Sure, rabbi. How will I know it's the books?"

"They're being sent from Dropsie College, and you will see that on the label." He nodded at the women and withdrew.

Myra Schwarz waited in martyred patience for Stanley to rejoin them. "It must have been pretty important for the rabbi to call you away," she remarked acidly.

"Oh, I was just coming down to shift the ladder anyway. He wanted me to keep an eye out for some books he's expecting."

"Very important," she said sarcastically. "His Holiness might be in for a little surprise one of these days."

"Oh, I don't think he saw us here when he first came in," said Emmy Adler.

"I don't see how he could help seeing us," said Mrs.

Drettman. Addressing herself to Myra, she went on, "You know, about what you were saying. My Morrie is a board of director, and only yesterday he got a call from Mr. Becker to make sure and turn up for this special meeting—"

Mrs. Schwarz gestured in the direction of Mrs. Adler. "That's supposed to be kept quiet," she whispered.

5

ALTHOUGH SHE WAS OFF AT NOON, ELSPETH RARELY MANaged to leave the Serafino household much before one. Mrs. Serafino made such a fuss about feeding the children their lunch—calling from the kitchen: "Oh El, where did you put Angelina's dish, the one with the three bears?" or "El, could you spare a minute before the bus leaves to put Johnnie on the toidy?"—that she usually preferred to do it herself and take the one o'clock bus or even the one-thirty.

Today in particular she didn't care, since her appointment was not until four. The day was hot and humid and she wanted to feel fresh and cool against the intimacy of the doctor's examination. She would have preferred to wait until three before leaving, but then her mistress might ask questions.

She was giving the children their lunch when Mrs. Serafino came downstairs. "Oh, you've started already," she said. "There was no need to. I'll finish and you can get dressed."

"They're almost through, Mrs. Serafino. Why don't you have your breakfast."

"Well, if you don't mind. I'm dying for a cup of coffee."

37

Mrs. Serafino was not one to turn down a favor, nor was she effusive in her thanks to the girl. It might give her ideas. When Elspeth had finished feeding the children, Mrs. Serafino was still at her coffee and made no move when she took them upstairs.

Preparing the children for their nap was as much of a chore as giving them lunch. When Elspeth finally came downstairs, Mrs. Serafino was in the hallway, talking on the telephone. She paused long enough to cup her hand over the mouthpiece. "Oh El, are the children already in bed? I was just coming up to do it." Just that, and back to her conversation.

Elspeth went to her room off the kitchen, closed the door, and firmly pushed the sliding bolt. She flung herself face down on the bed and automatically turned on the radio on the night table. She listened, only half-hearing, to the cheery voice of the announcer, "—and that was Bert Burns, the latest hillbilly sensation singing, 'Cornliquor Blues.' And now some news about the weather. That low-pressure area we mentioned earlier is moving closer and that means that we'll probably get some clouds and fog in the evening and maybe some showers. Well, I guess into every life some rain must fall, ha-ha. And now, for Mrs. Eisenstadt of 24 West Street, Salem, who is celebrating her eighty-third birthday, the Happy Hooligans in their latest platter, 'Trash Collection Rock.' And a happy birthday to you, Mrs. Eisenstadt."

She half-dozed through the song and then rolled over and stared at the ceiling through the one that followed, rebelling at the idea of having to get dressed in that humid warmth. Finally she got heavily to her feet and wiggled her dress over her head. She reached around behind and unhooked her bra and then unzipped her girdle and worked it down over her hips, not bothering to detach the stockings. She tossed the undergarments into the bottom drawer of her dresser and hung the dress in her closet.

Beyond the door, in the kitchen, she could hear that Mr. Serafino had come downstairs and was heating up the coffee and getting orange juice out of the refrigera-

38

tor. She glanced at the bolted door and then, reassured, went into the tiny bathroom and adjusted the shower.

When she emerged from her room half an hour later, she was wearing a sleeveless yellow linen dress, white shoes, white gloves, and carrying a white plastic handbag. Her short hair had been combed back severely and was held in place by a white elastic headband. Mr. Serafino had left, but his wife was in the kitchen, still in housecoat and mules, sipping at another cup of coffee.

"You look very nice, El," she said. "Something special tonight?"

"No, just a movie."

"Well, have a good time. You've got your key?"

The girl opened her bag to show the key attached to the zipper-pull of the change purse inside. Returning to her room, she closed the door behind her, went down a short hallway, and let herself out by the back door. She reached the corner just as the bus came along, and took a seat in the rear by an open window. As the bus started moving she removed her gloves and searched in her bag until she found a heavy, old-fashioned gold wedding band. She slid it on her finger and then drew her gloves on again.

When Joe Serafino returned to the kitchen, he was shaved and dressed.

"Has the girl gone yet?" he asked.

"You mean Elspeth? Yeah, she left a few minutes ago. Why?"

"I thought if she was going to Lynn, I could give her a ride in."

"Since when are you going to Lynn?"

"I've got to take the car in to the garage. The gadget that controls the top needs adjusting. The other day it got stuck in a rainstorm and went up only halfway and I got soaked."

"How come you waited until today to have it fixed?"

"I guess the weather has been so good I didn't think of it," he answered easily. "But I just heard the weather report while I was shaving and it said possible showers. Say, why the third degree?"

"No third degree. Can't a person ask a simple question? What time are you coming home, or maybe I shouldn't ask that either."

"Sure, go ahead and ask."

"Well?"

"I don't know—maybe I'll stay in Lynn and just grab a bite at the club." He sounded angry as he flung out of the room.

She heard the front door open and slam closed, and then the sound of the motor starting. She stared at the door of Elspeth's room and thought hard. Why should her husband, who usually acted as though he did not know the girl existed, suddenly want to be so obliging? For that matter, why did he get shaved at this hour? Ordinarily he waited until just before going to the club. His beard was so heavy that if he shaved earlier it showed before the evening was over.

The more she thought about it, the more suspicious the whole business seemed. Why, for example, did the girl hang around today? Her day off started at noon— why did she offer to feed the kids and then put them to bed? Nobody asked her to. No other girl would do it on her day off. She hadn't left until almost half-past two. Had she been waiting for Joe?

And that business of bolting the door. Up to now it had always amused her; whenever they had company and the conversation got around to maids, as it usually did, she would mention it. "Elspeth always bolts her door. I wonder if she thinks my Joe might come in while she's in bed or getting dressed." She always laughed when she said it as though the idea of her husband's being interested in the maid was completely ridiculous. But now she wondered if it was ridiculous. Could Elspeth be bolting it against her rather than against Joe? You could enter that room through the back way. Did Joe occasionally come in from the back, knowing that the door to the kitchen was bolted and they wouldn't be interrupted by his wife?

Another thought occurred to her. Although the girl had been with them over three months, she seemed to have no friends. All the other girls had dates on their days off. Why didn't she? Her only friend was that big horse of a girl, Celia, who worked for the Hoskins.

Could the reason Elspeth had no dates be that she was making beautiful music with her Joe?

She laughed at herself for her foolish suspicions. Why, she was with Joe practically all the time. She saw him at the club every night. Every night, that is, except Thursday. And Thursday was Elspeth's day off.

Several times Melvin Bronstein had reached for the telephone, and each time he withdrew his hand without removing the instrument from its cradle. Now it was after six and the staff had all gone home. Al Becker was still there but he was in his own office, and to judge by the books spread out on his desk, he was there to stay for a while.

He could call Rosalie undisturbed now. All week long she did not obtrude on his thoughts, but Thursdays when he was used to seeing her his need for her became overwhelming. In the year he had known her their relationship had settled down to a routine. Every Thursday afternoon she would call him and they would meet at some restaurant for dinner. Then they would drive out into the country and stop at a motel. He always brought her home by midnight, since the baby-sitter who took care of her children objected to staying later.

But recently there had been a change. He had not seen her last Thursday nor the Thursday before, because of her foolish fear that her estranged husband had hired detectives to watch her.

"Don't even call me, Mel," she had begged.

"But there can't be any harm in calling. You don't think they'd go to the trouble of tapping your telephone, do you?"

"No, but if we talk I might weaken. Then it will start all over again."

He had agreed because she had been insistent, and also because some of her fear had communicated itself to him. And now it was Thursday again. Surely he ought to call if only to inquire whether things had changed in any way. If only he could talk to her, he was sure that her need, which was as great as his, would overcome her fears.

Becker came into the room, making a great effort to

appear casual, and said: "Say, Mel, I almost forgot; Sally asked me to be sure and bring you home for dinner tonight."

Bronstein smiled to himself. Ever since Al and Sally had seen him with the girl a month ago, they had tried all kinds of stratagems to entice him to spend Thursday evenings with them.

"Gee Al, let me take a rain check, will you? I don't feel up to people tonight."

"Were you planning to eat at home?"

"No-o—Debbie's having her bridge club as usual. I thought I'd just grab a bite somewhere and then drop into a movie."

"Tell you what, kid, why don't you come over a little later, spend the evening with us. Sally just got some new records—highbrow stuff. We could listen to them and then go downstairs and shoot a couple of racks of pool."

"Well, if I drive by, perhaps I'll drop in."

Becker tried again. "Say, I've got a better idea. Why don't I call Sally and tell her I'm going to stay in town, and then the two of us could make a night of it—go some place for dinner, hoist a couple of drinks, and then take in a movie or go bowling?"

Bronstein shook his head. "Knock it off, Al. You go on home and have your dinner and relax. I'll be all right. Maybe I'll be over later."

He came around to the front of his desk and put his arm around the older man's shoulders. "Go on home, beat it. I'll lock up." Gently he led Becker to the door.

Then he picked up the telephone and dialed. He heard the phone ring at the other end, again and again and again. After a while he hung up.

It was late, after six, when the doctor finished his examination. Elspeth thanked the receptionist for the mimeographed diet and the booklet on pregnancy, and carefully folded and put them away in her purse. As she was about to leave, she asked if there was a public telephone in the building.

"There's one downstairs in the lobby, but you can use ours if you like."

Elspeth blushed shyly and shook her head. The receptionist thought she understood, and smiled.

In the phone booth she dialed a number, praying that he would be home. "It's me, dear, Elspeth," she said when she heard the voice at the other end. "I've got to see you tonight. It's terribly important."

She listened, and then said, "But you don't understand. There's something I've got to tell you . . . No, I can't over the phone . . . I'm in Lynn now, but I'm coming back to Barnard's Crossing. We could have dinner together. I thought I'd eat at the Surfside and then take in a movie at the Neptune."

She nodded as he answered, just as if he could see her. "I know you can't go to a movie with me tonight, but you have to eat so why can't we have dinner together? I'll be at the Surfside around seven. . . . Well, please try to make it . . . If you're not there by half-past seven I'll know that you couldn't come, but you will try, won't you?"

She stopped at a cafeteria before going on to the bus station. Sipping her coffee, she opened the booklet on pregnancy and read it through once and then again. When she was sure she understood the few simple rules, she tucked it behind the leather seat pad of the booth. It was too dangerous to keep; Mrs. Serafino might come across it.

6

AT HALF-PAST SEVEN JACOB WASSERMAN RANG THE BELL OF the rabbi's house. Mrs. Small answered the door. She was tiny and vivacious, with a mass of blonde hair that seemed to overbalance her. She had wide blue eyes and an open frank face that would have seemed ingenuous were they not offset by a firm, determined little chin.

"Come in, Mr. Wasserman, come in. It's so nice to see you."

Hearing the name, the rabbi, who had been engrossed in a book, came into the hall. "Why, Mr. Wasserman. We have just finished supper, but you'll have some tea, won't you? Make some tea, dear."

He led his visitor into the living room, while his wife went to set the water on. The rabbi placed the book he was holding face-down on the table beside him and looked inquiringly at the older man.

Wasserman suddenly realized that the rabbi's gaze, though mild and benign, was also penetrating. He essayed a smile. "You know, rabbi, when you first came to our congregation you suggested that you ought to sit in on the meetings of the board. I was all in favor of it. After all, if you engage a rabbi to help direct the development of a congregation, what's better than to have him sitting in on the meetings where the various activities are planned and discussed? But they voted me down. And do you know what their reason was? They said the rabbi is an employee of the congregation. Suppose we want to talk about his salary or his contract? How can we, if he's sitting right there with us? So what was the result? All year the matter wasn't even mentioned—until this last meeting. Then I suggested that we ought to decide about the contract for next year since there are only a couple of meetings left before we adjourn for the summer."

Mrs. Small came in with a tray. After serving them, she took a cup for herself and sat down.

"And what was decided about the contract?" asked the rabbi.

"We didn't decide anything," said Wasserman. "It was held over for the next meeting—that is, for this coming Sunday."

The rabbi studied his teacup, his brow furrowed in concentration. Then without looking up, as if thinking aloud, he said, "Tonight is Thursday, three days before the meeting. If approval were certain and the vote only a matter of form, you would have waited until Sunday to tell me. If approval were likely but not absolutely certain, you would probably mention it when next you happened to see me, which would be Friday evening at the services. But if it looked as though the vote were uncertain or even likely to go against me, you would not want to mention it Friday evening for fear of spoiling my Sabbath. So your coming tonight can only mean that you have reason to believe I will not be reappointed. That's it, isn't it?"

Wasserman shook his head in admiration. Then he turned to the rabbi's wife and waggled an admonishing forefinger. "Don't ever try to deceive your husband, Mrs. Small. He'll find you out in a minute." He turned back to the rabbi. "No, rabbi, that's not it, at least not exactly. Let me explain. We have forty-five members on the board of directors. Think of it! It's more than they have on the board of General Electric or United States Steel. But you know how it is, you put on the board anyone who is a little of a somebody; anyone who does a little work for the temple, or you think maybe he'll do some work for the temple, you put him on the board. It's an honor. Without meaning to, you usually end up with a board made up of the richer members of the congregation. Other temples and synagogues do the same thing. So of the forty-five, maybe fifteen come to every meeting. Then maybe ten more come every now and then. The rest, you don't see them from one year to the next. If only the fifteen regulars were to show up, we would win by a large majority, maybe as much as four to one. To most of us, it was merely a matter of form. We would have voted the contract right then and there. But we couldn't fight the motion to hold it over for a week. It seemed reasonable and it's what we do in all important decisions. But the opposition, Al Becker and his group, evidently had something else in mind. He doesn't like you, Al Becker. Just yesterday I found out that they went to work and phoned the thirty or so who don't come regular. And from what I can see, they didn't just argue the question with them. They put on whatever pressure they could. When I heard about it yesterday from Ben Schwarz, I began to contact these people myself, but I was too late, I found that most of them were already committed to Becker and his friends. That's how matters stand now. If we have the usual meeting with the usual members present, we'll have no trouble winning. But if he gets the whole board to attend . . ." He spread his hands, palms up, in token of defeat.

"I can't say that this comes as a complete surprise to me," the rabbi said ruefully. "My roots are in traditional Judaism, and when I entered the rabbinate, it was to become a rabbi of the sort my father was and my grandfather before him, to live the life of a scholar, not in seclusion, not in an ivory tower, but as part of the Jewish community, and somehow to influence it. But I'm beginning to think that there is no place for me or my kind in a modern American Jewish community. Congregations seem to want the rabbi to act as a kind of executive secretary, organizing clubs, making speeches, integrating the temple with the churches. Perhaps it's a good thing, perhaps I'm hopelessly out of fashion, but it's not for me. The tendency seems to be to emphasize our likeness to other denominations, whereas the whole weight of our tradition is to emphasize our differences. We are not merely another sect with minor peculiarities; we are a nation of priests, dedicated to God because He chose us."

Wasserman nodded his head impatiently. "But it takes time, rabbi. These people who make up our congregation grew up during the period between the two World Wars. Most of them never went to a cheder or even a Sunday school. How do you think it was when I first tried to organize a temple? We had fifty Jewish families here at the time, and yet when old Mr. Levy died, just to get a minyan so his family could say Kaddish—it was like pulling teeth. When we first started our temple, I went to see each and every Jewish family in Barnard's Crossing. Some of them had arranged car pools to take their kids to Sunday school in Lynn; some had a teacher come out to give their boys instruction for a few months so they could hold a Bar Mitzvah, and they used to phone back and forth to make arrangements to deliver him to the home of his next pupil. My idea was to establish a Hebrew school first, and use the same building for services for the holidays. Some thought it would cost too much money, and others didn't want their children to feel different by having them go to a special school in the afternoon.

"But little by little, I won them over. I got figures on costs, estimates, prices, plans, and then when we finally acquired a building, it was a wonderful thing. In the evenings, and Sundays, they used to come down—the women in slacks, the men in dungarees, everybody working together, cleaning, fixing, painting. There were no cliques then, no parties. Everybody was interested and everybody worked together. They didn't know very much, these young people. Most of them couldn't even say their prayers in Hebrew, but the spirit was there.

"I remember our first High Holiday services. I borrowed a Scroll from the Lynn synagogue, and I was the leader and the reader, and I even gave a little sermon. For the Day of Atonement, I had a little help from the principal of the Hebrew school, but most of it I did myself. It was quite a day's work, and on an empty stomach, too. I'm not a young man and I know my wife worried, but I never felt better in my life. It was a wonderful spirit we had in those years.''

"Then what happened?'' asked the rabbi's wife.

Wasserman smiled wryly. "Then we grew. Jews really began to come to Barnard's Crossing then. I like to think that our having a school and a temple had something to do with it. When there were only fifty families everybody knew everybody else, differences of opinion could be hammered out in personal discussion. But when you have three hundred or more families, as we have now, it's different. There are separate social groups now who don't even know each other. You take Becker and his group, the Pearlsteins and the Korbs and the Feingolds, those who live on Grove Point, they keep to themselves. Becker is not a bad man, you understand. In fact, he's a very fine man—and all those I mentioned, they're all fine people, but their point of view is different from yours and mine. From their point of view, the bigger, the more influential, the temple organization is, the better.''

"But they're the ones that pay the piper, so I suppose that gives them the right to call the tune,'' the rabbi remarked.

"The temple and the community are bigger than a few large contributors,'' said Wasserman. "A temple—''

He was interrupted by the doorbell, and the rabbi went to answer it. It was Stanley.

"You been waiting so anxious for those books, rabbi,'' he said, "that I thought I'd stop on my way home to tell you they came. It was a big wooden box, so I brought it up to your study and pried the lid off for you.''

The rabbi thanked him and returned to the living room. But he could barely conceal his excitement. "My books have come, Miriam.''

"I'm so glad, David.''

"You won't mind if I go over to look through them?'' Then he suddenly remembered his guest. "They're some rare books that were sent to me from the Dropsie College Library for a study I'm doing on Maimonides,'' he explained.

"I was just going, rabbi," said Wasserman, rising from his chair.

"Oh, you can't go now, Mr. Wasserman. You haven't finished your tea. You'll embarrass me if you leave now. Insist that he remain, Miriam."

Wasserman smiled good-naturedly. "I can see, rabbi, that you're anxious to get to your books and I don't want to keep you. Why don't you go on and I'll keep Mrs. Small company for a while."

"You're quite sure you don't mind?" But already he was heading for the garage.

His way was blocked by his wife, her firm little chin held high. "You will not leave this house, David Small," she announced, "unless you put on your topcoat."

"But it's mild out," he protested.

"By the time you get home, it will be quite chilly."

Resigned, the rabbi reached into the closet for his coat, but instead of putting it on he draped it defiantly over his arm.

Mrs. Small came back to the living room. "He's like a boy," she said by way of apology.

"No," said Mr. Wasserman. "I think maybe he wanted to be by himself for a while."

The Surfside was considered a reasonable restaurant: the prices were moderate, the service, though not fancy, was brisk and efficient, and although the decor was plain the food was good and the seafood exceptional. Mel Bronstein had never eaten there but as he approached, a car parked in front of the door pulled away and he took this as a sign. He remembered having heard the place well spoken of, and tooled his big blue Lincoln into the spot just vacated.

There were not too many people in the restaurant, he saw, as he made his way to a booth and ordered a martini. The walls were hung with lengths of fishnet, and other articles suggestive of the sea: a pair of oars, a mahogany ship's wheel, painted wooden lobster-trap floats, and occupying a wall to itself, a truly imposing swordfish mounted on a mahogany panel.

He glanced around and, not surprisingly, saw no one he knew. The Surfside was in the lower part of town,

Old Town, and people from his section, Chilton, rarely went there.

Most of the booths were occupied by couples, but diagonally across from him a young girl was, like himself, sitting alone. She was not pretty, but she had a young, fresh look. By the way she kept looking at her wristwatch he assumed she was waiting for someone; she had not ordered, but every now and then she sipped at her water glass, not because she was thirsty but because everyone else was eating.

The waitress came over to ask if he were ready to order, but he motioned to his glass to indicate a refill.

The girl opposite now seemed increasingly disturbed over the failure of her escort to appear. Each time she heard the door open, she turned around on her bench. Then, quite suddenly, her mood changed. She straightened up as if she had come to a decision. She drew off her white gloves and stuffed them into her handbag as though making ready to order. He saw she was wearing a wedding ring. As he watched, she twisted her ring off, opened her bag, and dropped it into the change purse.

She looked up and saw him watching her. Blushing, she turned away. He glanced at his watch. It was quarter to eight.

Hesitating only a moment, he eased out of the booth and went over to her. She looked up, startled.

"I am Melvin Bronstein," he said, "and quite respectable. I hate to eat alone and I imagine you do. Wouldn't you care to join me?"

Her eyes widened like a child's. For a moment she lowered them, and then she looked up at him again and nodded.

"Let me give you some more tea, Mr. Wasserman."

He inclined his head in thanks. "I can't tell you how badly I feel about this business, Mrs. Small. After all, I picked your husband; he was my personal choice."

"Yes, I know, Mr. Wasserman. We wondered about it at the time, David and I. Usually when a congregation wants to hire a rabbi they ask a number of candidates to come down on successive Sabbaths to conduct the services and to meet with the board of directors or with the ritual committee. But you came down to the seminary alone, and on your own responsibility you picked David." She eyed him speculatively and then immediately dropped her eyes to her teacup. "Perhaps if the ritual committee had acted as a whole they would have felt friendlier to him," she said quietly.

"You think perhaps I insisted on making the selection myself? Believe me, Mrs. Small, the responsibility was not of my choosing. I would have preferred to let the decision rest with the ritual committee or with the board, but the building was finished in early summer, and the board was determined to start the New Year in September completely organized. When I suggested that the ritual committee go down to New York in a body—there are only three of us: Mr. Becker, Mr. Reich, and myself—it was Mr. Becker, if you please, who insisted that I go alone. 'What do Reich and I know about rabbis, Jacob?' Those were his exact words. 'You know, so you go down and pick him. Anyone you choose will be all right with us.' Maybe he was busy and couldn't go out of town at the time, or maybe he really meant it. At first, I didn't want to take the whole responsibility. Then, when I thought it over, I decided maybe it would be for the best. After all, Reich and Becker, they really do know nothing. Becker can't even say his prayers in Hebrew, and Reich isn't much better. I had already had one lesson. When it came to awarding the contract for the construction of the temple they hired Christian Sorenson as the architect. A Jewish architect wouldn't do. If I hadn't spoken out, the name Christian Sorenson— Christian, mind you—would have been on a bronze plate on the front of the temple.

The renowned ecclesiastical architect, Christian Sorenson, an exquisite with a black silk artist's bow tie and pince-nez on a black ribbon to gesture with, had prepared a pasteboard model showing a tall, narrow box of a building with long narrow windows alternating with decorative columns of stainless steel. "I have spent the last fortnight in familiarizing myself with the basic tenets of your religion, gentlemen, and my design is intended to express its essential nature." (A gaon, Wasserman had thought, who can understand the essential

51

nature of Judaism in two weeks!) "You will note that the tall narrow lines give a sense of aspiration, calling as they do for an upward movement of the eyes; that the simplicity of the design, stark and unrelieved by any trumpery decoration"—(Was he referring to the traditional Jewish symbols: Star of David, seven-branched candelabrum, Tables of the Law?)—"typifies the practical simplicity, if I may say so, gentlemen, the basic common sense of your religion. The stainless steel columns suggest both the purity of the religion and its resistance to the decay and erosion of time."

The front elevation showed a row of stainless-steel doors from either side of which extended a long wall of glazed white brick that started at the full height of the doors and sloped away in a gentle curve to the extremities of the plot, "serving not only to soften the lines of the central mass, but also to relate it to the terrain. You will note that the effect is like a pair of open, embracing arms, calling upon people to come and worship. As a practical matter, these two walls, one on either side of the entrance, will separate the parking lot in front from the lawn which encircles the rest of the building."

"At least I was able to see that only his first initial is on the plate—and after all, it's not the building that forms the character of the congregation. But the character of the rabbi might. So I agreed to go down to the seminary alone."

"And why did you pick my David, Mr. Wasserman?"

He did not answer immediately. He realized that here was a very shrewd and forceful young woman and he should be careful with his answers. He tried to think just what it was that had attracted him to her husband. For one thing, he showed a considerable background in the study of the Talmud. No doubt the information in his folder, that he was descended from a long line of rabbis and that his wife was the daughter of a rabbi, had had something to do with it. Someone brought up in a rabbinical household could be expected to take the traditional, conservative point of view. But his first meeting had been disappointlng: the young rabbi's appearance was not imposing; he looked like a very ordinary young man. However, as they talked, he found himself beguiled by David Small's friendliness, by his common sense. Then there was something about his gestures and tone vaguely reminiscent of the bearded patriarch from whom he himself had learned the Talmud when a lad in the old country; the young man's voice had that gentle, coaxing quality, a certain rhythm that stopped just short of developing into the chant that was traditional with Talmudists.

Almost as soon as Wasserman had settled the matter, however, he had had misgivings. Not that he himself was dissatisfied, but he suspected that Rabbi Small was probably not what most of the congregation had in mind. Some expected a tall, austere man with a deep resonant voice, an Episcopal bishop sort of man; Rabbi Small was not tall, and his voice was gentle and mild and matter-of-fact. Some expected a jolly undergraduate sort of young man in gray flannels who would be at home on a golf course or at the tennis courts and be one with the young married set; Rabbi Small was thin and pale and wore eyeglasses, and although in excellent health he was obviously no athlete. Some had an image of the rabbi as a dynamic executive, an organizer, a go-getter who would set up committees, cajole or badger the entire congregation into ever more ambitious programs of service; Rabbi Small was rather absent-minded, had constantly to be reminded of his appointments, and had no idea of time or money. Although seemingly amenable to suggestions, he was also very good at forgetting them, especially if he had no great interest in them in the first place.

Wasserman picked his words carefully. "I'll tell you, Mrs. Small. I chose him partly because I liked him personally. But there was something else. As you know, I interviewed several others at the time. They were all fine boys with good smart Jewish heads on them. But a rabbi of a community has to be something more than just smart. He has to have courage and he has to have conviction. With each of them I sat and talked for a while. We talked about the function of the rabbi in the community. And each of them agreed with me. We were feeling each other out—you always do in this kind of an interview—and as soon as they thought they knew the general direction of my Jewishness they would give it to me as their view in much better form than I could put it. I said they were smart. But your husband didn't seem interested in finding out my views. And when I stated them, he disagreed with me, not disrespectfully, but quietly and firmly. An applicant for a job who disagrees with his prospective employer is either a fool or he has convictions, and there was nothing to suggest to me that your husband was a fool.

"And now, Mrs. Small, question for question: Why did your husband apply for the job and accept it when it was offered? I'm sure the placement office at the seminary gave the candidates some idea of the kind of community it was, and in my meeting with your husband I answered all his questions fairly."

"Your idea is that he should have tried for a position with a more settled community," she asked, "one likely to be more traditional in its practices and its attitude toward the rabbi?" She set her empty cup on the table. "We talked about it, and he felt that the future is not with them. Just to go along the established groove, just to mark time, that is not my David, Mr. Wasserman. He does have conviction, and he thought he could give it to your community. The fact that they sent a man like you, alone, to pick the rabbi, instead of a committee with the customary people like Mr. Becker, persuaded him that he had a chance. And now it appears that he was wrong. They definitely are planning to oust him?"

Wasserman shrugged his shoulders. "Twenty-one admit that they are going to vote against him. They're sorry, but they promised Al Becker or Dr. Pearlstein, or somebody else. Twenty say they'll vote for the rabbi. But of these, at least four I'm not so sure about. They might not show up. They promised me, but from the way they talked—'I've got to go out of town Saturday, but if I get back in time you can count on me.' So I can count on they won't come in Sunday morning, and when they see me later on, they'll tell me what a shame it is and how hard they tried to get back in time to come to the meeting."

"That's forty-one. What about the other four?"

"They'll think it over. That means that they've already made up their minds to vote against, but they didn't want me to argue with them. What can you say to someone who promises to think it over?—Don't think?''

"Well, if that's the way they want it—''

Suddenly Wasserman was angry. "How do they know what they want?'' he demanded. "When they first began to come here and I tried to get a congregation started— not even a congregation, more like a little club in case anything should happen, God forbid, we could arrange to have a minyan—this one said he didn't think he could spare the time and another one said he wasn't interested in organized religion, and several said they didn't think they could afford it. But I kept after them. If I had taken a vote and acted accordingly, would we have a temple with a cantor and a rabbi and a school with teachers?''

"But by your own figures, Mr. Wasserman, it's twenty-five, maybe even twenty-nine, out of forty-five.''

He smiled wanly. "So maybe I'm figuring with a black pencil. Maybe the ones who want to think it over, maybe they really haven't made up their minds. And Al Becker and Irving Feingold and Dr. Pearlstein, can they be so sure that everyone who promised them will come to the meeting? The outlook, it's not very bright, but a chance there is. And I'll be plain with you, Mrs. Small. Some of it is your husband's fault. There are many in the congregation, and I don't mean only Becker's friends, who feel that above all and most important, the rabbi is their personal representative in the community at large. And these people object to your husband's general attitude. They say it is almost as though he doesn't care. They say he's careless about his appointments, careless in his appearance, even careless in his manner in the pulpit. His clothes, they're apt to be wrinkled. When he gets up to speak in front of the congregation, or at a meeting, it doesn't look right.''

She nodded. "I know. And maybe some of these critics blame me. A wife should see to her husband. But what can I do? I see that his clothes are neat when he leaves in the morning, but can I follow him around all day? He's a scholar. When he gets interested in a book, nothing else matters. If he feels like lying down to read he doesn't bother to take off his jacket. When he's concentrating he runs his hands through his hair. So his hair gets mussed and he looks as if he just got up from sleep. When he's studying he makes notes on cards and puts them in his pockets, so that after a while they bulge. He's a scholar, Mr. Wasserman. That's what a rabbi is, a scholar. I know what you mean. I know the sort of man the congregation wants. He gets up in a public meeting to give the invocation. He bows his head as though the Almighty were right there in front of him. He shuts his eyes lest His Radiance should blind him, and then speaks in a low, deep voice—not the voice he uses in talking to his wife, but in a special voice, like an actor. My David is no actor. Do you think God is impressed by a low, deep voice, Mr. Wasserman?''

"Dear Mrs. Small, I'm not disagreeing with you. But we live in the world. This is what the world wants now in a rabbi, so this is what a rabbi has to be.''

"David will change the world, Mr. Wasserman, before the world will change my David.''

7

When Joe Serafino arrived at the club, he found a new hatcheck girl. He strolled over to the headwaiter, who acted as manager in his absence.

"Who's the new broad, Lennie?"

"Oh, I was going to tell you, Joe. Nellie's kid is sick again so I got this girl to stand in for her."

"What's her name?"

"Stella."

Joe looked her over. "She sure fills out that uniform," he admitted. "Okay, when things settle down, send her into the office."

"No funny business, Joe. No passes. She's like a distant cousin of my wife."

"Take it easy, Lennie. I got to get her name and address and Social Security, don't I?" Joe smiled. "You want I should bring the book out here?" He left to make his rounds of the dining room. Normally, he spent a good portion of the evening circulating among the customers, greeting one, waving to another, occasionally sitting down with one of the regulars to chat for a few minutes, after which he would snap his fingers at a passing waiter: "Give these good people a drink, Paul." But Thursday nights, maids' night out, the atmosphere was different. There were always a number of empty tables, and the people nursed their drinks, conversed in low voices, and seemed to lack spirit. Even the service was not the same; the waiters tended to huddle near the kitchen door instead of scurrying around filling orders. When Leonard glared at them or snapped his fingers to attract their attention, they would separate reluctantly, only to group together the moment his back was turned.

Thursdays, Joe spent much of the time in his office working on accounts. This evening he finished early and was trying to catch a brief nap on the couch when there was a knock on the door. He got up and seated himself at the desk with his account books open before him. "Come in," he said, in a gruff, businesslike tone.

He heard the doorknob turn ineffectually and then, smiling, he got up from his chair and turned back the night latch. He motioned the girl to the couch. "Siddown, kid," he said. "I'll be with you in a minute." Casually he pushed the door closed and returned to the swivel chair at the desk and frowned at the books in front of him. For a minute or two he appeared very busy, making little marks on paper and checking against the pages of his ledgers. Then he swung around and looked at her, letting his gaze wander slowly over her. "What's your name?"

"Stella, Stella Mastrangelo."

"How do you spell it? Never mind; here, write it down on this piece of paper."

She came to the desk and bent over to write. She was young and fresh, with a smooth olive skin and dark provocative eyes. His hand itched to pat her bottom, so enticingly encased in the black satin shorts of her uniform. But he had to play it cool, so in the same businesslike voice he said, "Put down your address and your Social Security. And you better put down your telephone number too, in case we want to get in touch with you in a hurry."

She finished writing and straightened up, but she did not immediately return to the couch. Instead, she leaned against the edge of the desk, facing him. "Is that all you want, Mr. Serafino?" she asked.

"Yeah." He studied the paper. "You know, we might

be able to use you from time to time. Nellie was hinting she'd like an extra night off. It'd give her more time with her kid."

"Oh, Mr. Serafino, I'd appreciate that."

"Yeah, well, we'll see about it. Say, you got your car here?"

"No, I came on the bus."

"Then how were you planning on getting home?"

"Mr. Leonard said I could leave just before midnight. That way I could catch the last bus."

"Aren't you afraid to go home that late at night alone? That's a hell of an arrangement. Tell you what, I'll drive you home tonight, and you can make some better arrangement next time. Pat, in the parking lot, can usually work out something for you with one of the cabbies."

"Oh, I couldn't have you do that, Mr. Serafino."

"Why not?"

"Well, Mr. Leonard said—"

He held up a hand. "Nobody has to know," he said, and his voice was easy and coaxing. "This door here leads right to the parking lot. You leave at quarter of twelve and walk down to the bus stop and wait for me there. I'll get my car and pick you up."

"But Mr. Leonard—"

"Lennie wants to see me, he comes here. He finds the door locked and he knows I'm grabbing a little shut-eye. He knows better than to disturb me when I'm having a little snooze. Okay? Besides, we got business to talk about, ain't we?"

She nodded her head and fluttered her eyelashes at him.

"Okay, run along, kid, and I'll see you later." He patted her in dismissal, in a fatherly sort of way.

The Ship's Cabin served sandwiches, doughnuts, and coffee during the day. In the evening they offered hot dishes—spaghetti and meatballs, fried clams and french fried potatoes, baked beans and frankforts—which were described on greasy, flyspecked cards and inserted in the frame of the bar mirror. Each dish was numbered and regulars like Stanley would order by number, presumably to speed up the operation.

There was no heavy drinking either during the day or in the early evening. The patrons who dropped in at midday usually took ale or beer to wash down their sandwich. Those who came later might have a shot of whiskey before supper. But the regular customers, like Stanley, usually returned around nine. That was when the Ship's Cabin really came alive.

After leaving the rabbi's house, Stanley drove his yellow jalopy to the Ship's Cabin, had his regular evening meal, one of the three specials, together with a few glasses of ale. He sat at the bar eating stolidly, his jaws moving rhythmically like a machine. He focused on his plate just long enough to load his fork and then turned his head to watch the television screen set high in one corner of the room, as he chewed away. Every now and then, he reached for his glass and took a long draught, his eyes remaining fixed on the screen.

Except for exchanging a remark about the weather with the bartender when he first set his plate before him, Stanley spoke to no one. The program ended, and he drained the remains of his second glass, wiped his mouth with the paper napkin that had lain folded all through supper, and ambled over to the cashier to pay his tab.

He left the tavern with a wave to the bartender, and drove the few blocks to Mama Schofield's. No point in hanging around; there would be nothing doing for another hour or two.

Mrs. Schofield was sitting in her parlor when he stuck his head in to say good evening. Upstairs in his room he took off his shoes, his denim work pants and shirt, and lay down on the bed, his hands clasped under his head, staring up at the ceiling. There were no pictures like those he had on the wall in the temple basement; Mama Schofield would not have stood for them. The only decoration was a calendar showing a picture of a little boy and a puppy that was somehow supposed to induce fond feelings for the Barnard's Crossing Coal Company.

Usually he napped for an hour or so, but tonight for some reason he was restless. He realized he was undergoing one of his frequent attacks of loneliness. In his circle of acquaintances, his bachelorhood was regarded as proof that he was too smart to have got himself caught. He wondered uneasily if he hadn't outsmarted himself. What sort of life did he have? Supper, a greasy meal eaten at a counter stool; then back to a furnished room, with the boozy good fellowship of the Ship's Cabin afterward the only thing to look forward to. If he were married now—and his mind slipped into a pleasant daydream of married life. Soon he dozed off.

When he awoke, it was almost ten o'clock. He got up and dressed in his good clothes and drove to the Ship's Cabin. The dream persisted. He drank more than usual in an effort to drown it, but it only bobbed up whenever the talk lagged or the noise momentarily abated.

Toward midnight the crowd began to thin out and Stanley got up to go. The loneliness was stronger than ever. He realized that it was Thursday and there probably would be some girl getting off the last bus at Oak and Vine. Maybe she would be tired and appreciate the offer of a ride the rest of the way home.

Elspeth sat in the back seat of the car. The rain had let up somewhat, but large drops still bounced on the asphalt, turning it into a sleek black pool. She was at ease now, and to prove it she took slow, graceful puffs at her cigarette, like an actress. When she spoke, she stared straight ahead, only occasionally darting quick looks at her companion to see how he was reacting.

He was sitting bolt upright, his eyes wide and unwinking, his jaw set and his lips tight—in anger? in frustration? in despair? She could not tell. She leaned forward to snuff her cigarette in the ashtray attached to the back of the front seat. Very deliberately, as if to emphasize each word, she tapped her cigarette out against the little metal snuffer.

She sensed, rather than saw, his hand reaching forward. She felt it on her neck and was about to turn to smile at him when his fingers curled around her silver choke collar. She tried to complain he was holding too tight but his hand gave the heavy chain a sudden twist, and it was too late—too late to remonstrate—too late to cry out. The cry was stifled in her throat and she was enveloped in a red mist. And then there was blackness.

He sat with his arm still outstretched, his hand gripping the silver choker as one would to restrain a vicious dog. After a while he relaxed his grip, and as she began to fall forward he caught her by the shoulder and eased her onto the seat again. He waited. Then, cautiously, he opened the door of the car and looked out. Certain that there was no one in sight, he got out, and leaning in, scooped her up in his arms and eased her out of the car. Her head lolled back.

He did not look at her. With a swing of his hip, he slammed the door to. He carried her over to the wall where it was lowest, barely three feet high. Leaning over, he tried to set her down gently on the grass on the other side, but she was heavy and rolled out of his arms. He reached down in the darkness to close her eyes against the rain, but it was her hair that he felt. There seemed to be no point in trying to turn her over.

8

THE ALARM CLOCK ON THE NIGHT TABLE BESIDE RABBI
Small's bed rang at a quarter to seven. That gave him
time to shower, shave, and dress for morning services at
the temple at seven-thirty.

He reached and turned off the alarm, but instead of
getting up he made happy animal sounds and rolled over
again. His wife shook him. "You'll miss services, David."

"This morning I'm going to pass them up."

She thought she understood and did not insist. Besides, she knew he had come in very late the night
before, long after she had gone to bed.

Later, in his study, Rabbi Small was reciting the morning prayer, while in the kitchen Miriam was preparing
his breakfast. When she heard his voice raised exul-
tantly in the Shema: Hear O Israel, the Lord is our God,
the Lord is One, she began heating the water; when she
heard the buzz-buzz of the Amidah, she started his
eggs, cooking them until she heard him chant the Alenu,
when she took them out of the boiling water.

He came out of the study a few minutes later, rolling
down the left sleeve of his shirt and buttoning the cuff.
As always, he looked with dismay at the table set for
him.

"So much?"

"It's good for you, dear. Everybody says that breakfast is the most important meal of the day." Her mother-in-law had been most insistent on it: "You should see that he eats, Miriam. Don't ask him what he wants, because for him, if he has a book propped up in front of him or if he has some idea spinning around in his head, he can gnaw on a crust of bread and be satisfied. You've got to see that he eats regular, a balanced diet with lots of vitamins."

Miriam had already breakfasted—toast and coffee and a cigarette—so she hovered over him, seeing to it that he finished his grapefruit, setting his cereal down before him with an air that indicated she would brook no refusal. As soon as he had finished the last spoonful, she served his eggs, along with his toast already buttered. The trick was to avoid any delay during which his mind could wander and he would lose interest. Not until he had started on his eggs and toast did she pour herself another cup of coffee and permit herself to sit down opposite him.

"Did Mr. Wasserman stay long after I left?" he asked.

"About half an hour. I think he feels I should take better care of you, see that your suits are always pressed and your hair combed."

"I should be more careful of my appearance. Am I all right now? No egg stains on my tie?" he asked anxiously.

"You look fine, David. But you can't seem to stay that way." She regarded him critically. "Maybe if you used one of those collar pins, your tie would stay in place."

"You need a shirt with a special collar for that," he said. "I tried one once. It binds my throat."

"And couldn't you use some of that stuff that keeps your hair in place?"

"You want women to chase me? Would you like that?"

"Don't tell me you're above wanting to be attractive to women."

"You think that would do it?" he asked in mock eagerness. "A shirt with a tab collar and stickum on my hair?"

"Seriously, David, it is important. Mr. Wasserman seemed to think it was very important. Do you think they'll drop your contract?"

He nodded. "Quite probably. I'm sure he wouldn't have come down to see us yesterday if he thought otherwise."

"What will we do?"

He shrugged his shoulders. "Notify the seminary that I am at liberty and have them find me another congregation."

"And if the same thing happens again?"

"We notify them again." He laughed. "You remember Manny Katz, Rabbi Emmanuel Katz, the one with that tomboy wife? He lost three jobs one right after the other because of her. She used to wear shorts around the house during the summer, and when they went to the beach she wore a bikini, which is exactly what the women her age in the congregation would wear. But what they tolerated in their young women they wouldn't tolerate in the rebbitzin. And Manny wouldn't ask his wife to change. He finally got a job with a congregation down in Florida, where I guess everybody dresses that way. He's been there ever since."

"He was lucky," she said. "Do you expect to strike a congregation where the leaders wear sloppy clothes and are absent-minded and don't keep their appointments?"

"Oh, probably not. But when we get tired wandering, I can always get a job teaching. Nobody cares how teachers dress."

"Why don't we do that right away instead of waiting to be kicked out of half a dozen congregations? I'd like to be a teacher's wife. You could get a job at some college in Semitics, maybe even at the seminary. Just think, David, I wouldn't have to worry whether the president of the Sisterhood approved of my housekeeping or if the president of the local Hadassah thought my dress was in good taste."

The rabbi smiled. "Only the dean's wife. And I wouldn't have to attend community breakfasts."

"And I wouldn't have to smile every time a member of the congregation looked in my direction."

"Do you?"

"Of course. Till my face muscles ache. Oh let's do it, David."

He looked at her in surprise. "You're not serious." His face turned sober. "Don't think I don't feel my failure here, Miriam. It bothers me, not merely failing at something that I set out to do, but knowing that the congregation needs me. They don't know it yet, but I know it. Without me, or someone like me, you know what happens to these congregations? As religious institutions, that is, as Jewish religious institutions, they dry up. I don't mean that they're not active. As a matter of fact, they become veritable hives of activity with dozens of different groups and clubs and committees—social groups and art groups and study groups and philanthropy groups and athletic groups, most of them ostensibly Jewish. The dance group works up an interpretive dance they call Spirit of the Israeli Pioneer; the choral group adds 'White Christmas' to its repertoire so they can sing it at Christian churches during Brotherhood Week and the church can respond by having its lead tenor sing 'Eli, Eli.' The rabbi conducts the holiday services with great decorum, and except for an occasional responsive reading he and the cantor perform the entire service between them. You would never know that this is the spiritual home of a people who for three thousand years or more considered themselves a nation of priests sworn to the service of God, because every bit of the energy of the congregation and the rabbi too will be bent on showing that this Jewish church is no different from any other church in the community."

The doorbell rang. Miriam opened the door to a stocky man with a pleasant Irish face and snow-white hair.

"Rabbi David Small?"

"Yes?" The rabbi looked at him inquiringly, then at the card that indicated he was Hugh Lanigan, chief of police of Barnard's Crossing.

"Can I talk to you privately?" he asked.

"Of course." The rabbi led the way to his study. He closed the door, asking his wife as he did so to see that they were not interrupted.

Motioning his visitor to a chair, he sat down himself and looked at his guest expectantly.

"Your car was parked in the temple parking lot all night, rabbi."

"This is not permitted?"

"Of course. The parking lot is private property, and I guess if anyone has a right it would be you. As a matter of fact, we don't usually fuss too much if a car is parked on the street all night unless it's winter and there's a snowstorm and it interferes with the plows."

"So?"

"So we wondered why you left it there instead of in your own garage?"

"Did you think someone might steal it? It's very simple. I left it at the temple because I did not have the keys to drive it off with." He smiled, a little embarrassed. "That's not too clear, I'm afraid. You see, I went to the temple last night and spent the evening in my study. Some books had arrived that I was anxious to look over. Then, when I left, I closed the door of the study, and that locked it. You understand?"

Lanigan nodded. "Spring latch on the door."

"All my keys, including the key to the temple study, were on a key ring on my desk inside. I couldn't open the door of the study to get them, so I had to walk home. Does this explain the mystery?"

Lanigan nodded reflectively. Then, "I understand you people have prayers every morning. This morning you did not go, rabbi."

"That's right. There are some members of my congregation who take it amiss if their rabbi skips a daily service, but I hardly expected them to lodge a complaint with the police."

Lanigan laughed shortly. "Oh, nobody complained. At least, not to me, not in my capacity as police chief—"

"Come, Mr. Lanigan, evidently something has happened, a police matter in which my car is concerned—no, I myself must be concerned or you wouldn't want to know why I didn't go to morning prayers. If you will tell me what happened, perhaps I can tell you what you wish to know, or at least be able to help you more intelligently."

"You're right, rabbi. You understand that we're bound by regulations. My common sense tells me that you as a man of the cloth are in no way implicated, but as a policeman—"

"As a policeman you are not supposed to use your common sense? Is that what you were going to say?"

"That's not far from the truth! And yet there's good reason for it. We are bound to investigate everyone who could be involved, and although I know a rabbi would be no more likely to commit the sort of crime we're investigating than a priest, we've got to check everyone through."

"I would not presume to suggest what a priest would or would not do, chief, but anything that a man might do a rabbi might do. We are no different from ordinary men. We are not even men of the cloth, as you call it. I have no duties or privileges that any member of my congregation does not have. I am only presumed to be learned in the Law by which we are enjoined to live."

"It's kind of you to put it on that footing, rabbi. I'll be candid with you. This morning, the body of a young woman of nineteen or twenty was found on the temple grounds right behind the low wall that divides the parking lot from the lawn. She had evidently been killed sometime during the night. We'll have a pretty good idea of the time when the laboratory gets through checking."

"Killed? An accident?"

"Not an accident, rabbi. She was strangled with a silver chain that she wore around her neck, one of those heavy link chains with a locket. No chance of it being an accident."

"But this is terrible. Was it—was it a member of my congregation? Someone I know?"

"Do you know an Elspeth Bleech?" asked the chief.

The rabbi shook his head. "It's an unusual name, Elspeth."

"It's a variation of Elizabeth, of course. It's English and the girl was from Nova Scotia."

"From Nova Scotia? A tourist?"

Lanigan smiled. "Not a tourist, rabbi, a domestic. You know, during the Revolution a number of the more important and wealthier citizens of the Colonies, especially right here in Massachusetts, ran off to Canada, mostly to Nova Scotia. Loyalists, they were called. And now their descendants come back down here to go into domestic service. Pretty bad guessing on the part of their ancestors. This one worked for the Serafinos. Do you know the Serafinos, rabbi?"

"The name sounds Italian." He smiled. "If I have any Italians in my congregation, I'm not aware of it."

Lanigan grinned back at him. "They're Italians all right, and I know they don't go to your church because they go to mine, the Star of the Sea."

"You're Catholic? That surprises me, by the way. I didn't think of Barnard's Crossing as the sort of town where a Catholic was apt to get to be chief of police."

"There have been a few Catholic families here since the Revolution. Mine was one of them. If you knew the history of the town, you'd know that this is one of the few communities in Puritan Massachusetts where a Catholic could live in peace. The town was started by a group that didn't care too much about Puritanism."

"That's very interesting. I must investigate it someday." He hesitated, then he said, "The girl—had she been attacked or molested?"

Lanigan spread his hands in a gesture of ignorance. "Seemingly not, but the medical examiner might come up with something. There were no signs of struggle, no scratches, no torn clothing. On the other hand, she wasn't wearing a dress—just a slip, with a light topcoat and one of those transparent plastic raincoats over that. From what we have right now, there are no signs of struggle. The poor girl didn't have a chance. This chain she was wearing is what they call a choker, I believe. It closely encircles the neck. The murderer had only to grab it in back and twist."

"Terrible," the rabbi murmured, "terrible. And you think this was done on temple grounds?"

Lanigan pursed his lips. "We're not sure where it happened. For all we know, she could have been killed elsewhere."

"Then why was she brought there?" asked the rabbi, ashamed that his mind automatically reverted to thoughts of a scheme to discredit the Jewish community with some fantastic plot of ritual murder.

"Because, when you come to think of it, it's not a bad

69

place for the purpose. You might think that out here in the suburbs there'd be any number of places where you could dispose of a body, but actually there aren't. Most of the likely places are apt to be under someone's view. Places where there are no houses tend to become lovers' lanes. No, I'd say the temple area would be one of the best spots. It's dark, there are no houses in the immediate vicinity, and there's not likely to be anyone around most nights." He paused and then said, "By the way, between what times were you there?"

"You are wondering if I heard or saw anything?"

"Ye-es."

The rabbi smiled. "And you would also like to know how I was myself engaged during the critical time. Very well. I left my house around half-past seven or eight o'clock. I'm not sure of the time because I don't have the habit of glancing at my watch. Most of the time I don't bother to wear one. I had been having tea with my wife and Mr. Wasserman, the president of our congregation, when Stanley—he's our janitor—stopped by to tell me that a box of books I had been expecting had arrived and was now in my study. I excused myself and got into my car and drove to the temple. I left only minutes after Stanley left, so between my wife and Mr. Wasserman and Stanley you should be able to get pretty close to the exact time. I parked my car and let myself into the temple and went directly to my study on the second floor. I stayed until after twelve. I know that because I happened to glance at the clock on my desk and saw that it was midnight and decided I should be getting back. I was in the middle of a chapter, however, so I didn't leave immediately." He had a sudden idea. "This might help you to fix the time with greater precision: just before I arrived home, there was a sudden cloudburst and I had to sprint the rest of the way. I suppose somebody, the weather bureau perhaps, keeps an accurate record of the weather."

"That was at 12:45. We checked that first thing because the girl was wearing a raincoat."

"I see. Well, normally it takes me twenty minutes to walk from the temple to my house. I know because we do it every Friday evening and Saturday. But I think I walked more slowly last night. I was thinking of the books I had read.''

"But on the other hand, you ran part of the way.''

"Oh, that was just the last hundred yards or so. Call it twenty-five minutes and I think that would be fairly accurate. That would mean that I left the temple at twenty past.''

"Did you meet anyone on the way?''

"No, just the police officer. I suppose he knew me because he said good evening.''

"That would be Officer Norman.'' He smiled. "He wouldn't have to know you to say good evening. He rings in at one o'clock at the box on Vine Street just beyond the temple. I'll be able to get the time from him when I see him.''

"You mean he records it?''

"Probably not, but he'll remember. He's a pretty good man. Now, when you entered the temple, you turned on the light, I suppose.''

"No, it wasn't dark yet.''

"But you turned on the light in your study of course.''

"Of course.''

"So that anyone passing by would have seen it.''

The rabbi considered. Then he shook his head. "No, I turned on my desk lamp rather than the overhead light. I opened the window, of course, but I lowered the venetian blind.''

"Why?''

"Frankly, so that I wouldn't be interrupted. A member of the congregation might pass by and see the light and come up to chat.''

"So no one approaching the temple would guess anyone was there. Is that right, rabbi?''

The rabbi thought a moment and then nodded.

The police chief smiled.

"This has some significance for you?''

"Well, it might help to clarify the time element. Suppose the light could be seen. Then that, in conjunction with your car in the parking lot, would indicate that someone was still in the building and might come out at any time. If that were the case, it would be fair to assume the body had been deposited behind the wall

71

after you left. But with no light showing, it might be assumed your car had been left for the night perhaps because you couldn't get it started. Under those circumstances, the body could have been dropped while you were still upstairs. Now the medical examiner's first estimate was that the girl was killed around one o'clock. At this point in his examination, that's just an educated guess. If your light had been visible, it would tend to corroborate his estimate, but since the light could not be seen the girl could have been dropped near the wall while you were in your study, and that could have been anytime from the early evening on."

"I see."

"Now think carefully, rabbi, did you hear or see anything unusual—a cry? the sound of an automobile driving onto the parking lot?"

The rabbi shook his head.

"And you saw no one either while you were in your study or on your way home?"

"Only the police officer."

"Now you say you do not know Elspeth Bleech. Is it possible that you know her but not by name? After all, she lived with the Serafinos no great distance from the temple."

"It is possible."

"A girl of nineteen or twenty, blonde, about five feet four, a little on the stocky side but not unattractive. Perhaps later I'll be able to show you a picture."

The rabbi shook his head. "I don't recognize her from your description. It would fit many girls I may have seen. Nothing comes to mind at the moment, however."

"Well, let me put it this way: did you give anyone a lift in your car in the last day or two who might answer that description?"

The rabbi smiled and shook his head. "A rabbi, no less than a priest or a minister, finds it necessary to be circumspect about those things. I would be no more likely to offer a lift to a strange young woman then they would. One's congregation might misinterpret it. No, I gave no one a lift."

"Could your wife perhaps?"

"My wife doesn't drive."

Lanigan rose and held out his hand. "You've been very cooperative, rabbi, and I appreciate it."

"Any time."

At the door, Lanigan paused. "I hope you won't be needing your car for a little while. My boys are checking it over."

The rabbi looked his surprise.

"You see, the girl's handbag was found in it."

9

HUGH LANIGAN KNEW STANLEY, JUST AS HE KNEW ALL THE Old Towners. He found him working in the vestry, setting up a long table on which the Sisterhood would later serve the little cakes and tea things that constituted the usual collation after the Friday evening service.

"Just checking on this business, Stanley."

"Sure, Hugh, but I told Eban Jennings all I know."

"Well, you might as well give it to me again. You went to the rabbi's house last night to tell him about a box of books. When did the books arrive?"

"Delivered by Robinson's Express around six o'clock. Maybe a little after. It was his last stop."

"And when did you go over to the rabbi's?"

"Seven-thirty or so. I got this box and it's a pretty big wooden case and it's for the rabbi. I don't know that it's books at first—I mean, the rabbi, he told me about a shipment of books he was expecting, but I had no idea it would come in a wooden box. But then I notice it was shipped from Dropsie College. Well, the rabbi had mentioned that the books were coming from Dropsie College. Now that's a funny name for a college, and I remembered it because my Aunt Mattie—you remember her—well, that's what she had, dropsy, I mean. She was all puffed up, you could hardly see her eyes—"

"Never mind, just tell me about the box."

"Oh yeah, so I see the name and I remember that that's where the books were supposed to come from. So I figure it must be the books. Well, you wouldn't believe it, Hugh, but this rabbi—he's a nice feller and all that—but he wouldn't know which end of a hammer you hit with. So no matter what's in that case, I'm going to have to open it for him anyway. Right? So I figured I might as well do it right then. So I toted the whole business, box and all—and it was heavy as a sonofabitch, Hugh—right up to his study. Then I kind of finished my chores here and I thought I'd let him know that they came, seeing as he was so anxious for them and it was on my way home anyway."

"Where you living now, Stanley?"

"I got a room at Mama Schofield's."

"Didn't you used to live at the temple?"

"Yeah, at the old place. I had me a room up in the attic. Beauty. It was kind of nice, living right at the job, you know. But then they stopped it. They gave me a few bucks more each month to pay for a room, and I've been at Mama Schofield's ever since."

"Why did they stop it?" asked Lanigan.

"I'll tell you the truth, Hugh. They found out I was having some company up there once in a while. No wild parties, you understand, Hugh. I wouldn't do anything like that, and never while the temple was being used. Just a couple of people over for a little talk and a few beers. But I guess they got to thinking I might take it into my head to bring a broad up there, maybe on one of their holy days." He gave a loud chortle and slapped his thigh. "I suppose they were afraid that while they were praying down below, I might be bouncing a broad upstairs, and that would kind of short-circuit their prayers on the way up, see?"

"Go on."

"So they asked me to find myself a room, and I did. There was no hard feelings."

"How about here in the new building? Don't you ever sleep over?"

"Well, in the winter after a heavy snowfall, when I got to get the sidewalks cleared early. I got me a cot down in the boiler room."

"Let's go take a look at it."

"Sure, Hugh." Stanley led the way down a short flight of iron stairs and then stood aside as Lanigan pushed open a steel-clad fire door. The boiler room was immaculate, except for the corner where Stanley had set up his cot. Lanigan pointed out that the blankets were rumpled.

"Been that way since the last snowfall?" he asked.

"I lie down for a nap most afternoons," said Stanley easily. He watched while Lanigan poked idly through the cigarette butts in the ashtray. "I told you I never have anybody down here."

Lanigan sat down in the wicker chair and let his eyes wander over Stanley's art gallery. Stanley grinned sheepishly.

The police chief motioned for him to sit down, and he obediently plumped down on the cot. "Now let's get on with it. Around half-past seven you stopped at the rabbi's house to tell him about the box. Why couldn't you wait until morning? Did you expect the rabbi to leave his house at night?"

Stanley showed surprise at the question. "Why sure, the rabbi is up there reading and studying plenty of nights."

"Then what did you do?"

"I went on home."

"Stop on the way?"

"Sure, I stopped at the Ship's Cabin for a bite of supper and a couple of beers. Then I went on to Mama Schofield's."

"And you stayed there?"

"Yeah, I was there all the early evening."

"And then you went to bed?"

"Well, I went out for a beer just before turning in. At the Ship's Cabin it was."

"And what time did you leave this time?"

"Maybe around midnight. Maybe a little later."

"And you went right home to Schofield's?"

For a moment he hesitated, then, "Uh-huh."

"Anybody see you come in?"

"No, why should they? I got my own key."

"All right. What time did you come to work this morning?"

"Same as always. A little before seven."

"And what did you do?"

"They have a service here at half-past seven in the chapel. So I put on the lights and open a couple of windows to kind of air the place out. Then I set about my regular work, which this time of year it's mostly working on the lawn. I been raking up grass clippings mostly. I started yesterday working on the Maple Street side. So I started where I left off and gradually worked my way around the back of the building and then around to the other side. That's when I saw the girl. They were just coming out of the service and getting in their cars when I spotted her up against the brick wall. I walked over and I could see she was dead. I looked over the wall and Mr. Musinsky—he's a regular, I mean he comes every morning—he hadn't got in his car yet, so I hailed him. He took a look and then went right back into the temple to call you people."

"Did you notice the rabbi's car when you arrived this morning?"

"Oh sure."

"Surprised?"

"Not particularly. I figured he had come for morning prayers and had just got there early. When I saw he wasn't in the chapel, I figured he was in his study."

"You didn't go up to look?"

"No, what would I do that for?"

"All right." Lanigan rose and Stanley did likewise. The police chief strode out into the corridor with Stanley right behind him. He turned his head and said matter-of-factly, "You recognized the girl, of course."

"No," Stanley said quickly.

Lanigan turned around to face him. "You mean you never saw her before?"

"You mean this girl that was—"

"What other girl are we talking about?" asked Lanigan coldly.

"Well, working around the temple here, naturally I

77

see a lot of people. Yes, I seen her around. I mean, I've seen her walking with those two little dago kids she takes care of."

"Did you know her?"

"I just said I seen her." Stanley sounded exasperated.

"Did you ever make a pass at her?"

"Why would I do that?" demanded Stanley.

"Because you're as horny as a mink."

"Well, I didn't."

"Ever talk to her?"

Stanley drew a dirty handkerchief from a pocket of his dungarees and began to mop his forehead.

"What's the matter, feeling warm?"

Stanley exploded. "Goddammit, Hugh, you're trying to get me tied up in this. Sure I talked to her. I'm standing around and a young chick comes along with a couple of kids in tow and one of them starts pulling at the shrubbery, naturally I'm going to speak up."

"Naturally."

"But I never went out with her or anything."

"Never showed her that little pigpen you've got down in the basement?"

"Just, Hello or It's a nice morning, isn't it?" said Stanley doggedly. "And half the time, she never even answered."

"I can imagine. All right, how did you know the kids were Italian?"

"Because I seen them with their father, Serafino, and I knew him because I once did some work on his house."

"When was this?"

"When did I see him? A couple or three days ago maybe. He drove up in his convertible and he sees the girl and the kids and he asks do they want their daddy should get them some ice cream. Then they all pile into the front seat, the girl and then the kids fighting about who was going to sit next to the door, and the girl wiggling over to make room and the old man kind of arsing her. Disgusting."

"Disgusting because it wasn't you?"

"Well, at least I'm free and not a married man with a couple of kids."

10

IT HAD BEEN A HECTIC MORNING FOR THE SERAFINOS. AL-
though Mrs. Serafino went to bed early on Thursday
nights, she did not usually rise much before ten on
Fridays. But this morning she had been awakened by
the children, who, having pounded on Elspeth's door to
no effect, burst into her bedroom demanding to be
dressed.

Angry at the girl for oversleeping, she wrapped a robe
about her and went down to wake her up. She pounded
on the door and called her name. When the girl failed to
respond, it occurred to her that Elspeth might not be in
her room, and that could only mean she had not come
home at all last night. For a live-in maid, this was a
cardinal offense punishable by immediate dismissal. She
was about to run outside to peer through the window
and confirm her suspicions when the front doorbell rang.

She was so certain it was Elspeth, probably with some
cock-and-bull story about having lost her key, that she
raced down the hall and flung open the front door. It
was a uniformed policeman. Her robe had fallen open,
and for a moment she just stood there staring at him
stupidly. His blush of embarrassment suddenly made

her realize that she was exposed, and she hastily gathered the garment about her.

There followed a nightmare of a morning. Other policemen came, in and out of uniform. The telephone rang incessantly, all police business. She was told to get her husband up and dressed so that he could accompany one of the officers to make formal identification of the body.

"Couldn't I identify her?" she asked. "My husband needs his sleep."

"He's a good man if he can sleep through all this," said the officer, and then not unkindly, "Believe me, lady, you better have him do it. She's not very pretty."

Somehow the children managed to get fed and dressed, and she even prepared a breakfast of sorts for herself. And all the time she was eating there were questions: formal interrogations with one officer sitting across the table and another taking notes; questions while they were measuring and photographing the girl's room; questions asked abruptly as if to take her by surprise.

After a while they left. The children were out in the backyard for the moment, and she had decided to lie down on the couch for a few minutes of relaxation, when the doorbell rang once again. It was Joe.

She scanned his face anxiously. "Was it the girl?"

"Sure it was the girl. Who else would it be? You think the cops didn't know who it was before I identified her?"

"Then why did they need you?"

"Because it's the law, that's why. It's like a routine you got to go through."

"Did they ask you any questions, Joe?"

"Cops always ask questions."

"Like what? What did they ask you?"

"Like did she have any enemies? What was the name of her boyfriend? Who were her friends? Was she upset lately? When was the last time I saw her?"

"And what did you tell them?"

"What do you think I told them? I told them I didn't know of no boyfriend, that this girl Celia who works for the Hoskins is the only girlfriend she's got I know of, that she looked all right to me and I didn't see no signs of her being upset."

"And did you tell them when was the last time you saw her?"

"Sure, it was around one-two o'clock yesterday. Jesus, what's all this questioning? I get it from the cops and then I come home and get it from you. And all morning, I haven't even had a cup of coffee yet?"

"I'll get you some coffee, Joe. Would you like some toast with it? Eggs? Cereal?"

"No, just coffee. I'm all wound up—my stomach it's all tied up in knots."

She went about heating the coffee. Without turning she asked, "Which was it, one or two o'clock, that you last saw her, Joe?"

He canted his head at the ceiling. "Let's see, I came down and had my breakfast—around noon, wasn't it? I saw her then. I guess I did—" uncertainly. "Anyway, I heard her giving the kids their lunch and then getting them ready for their nap. Then I went up to get dressed and by the time I came back she was already gone."

"You didn't see her after that?"

"What do you mean? What the hell are you driving at?"

"Well, you were going to give her a ride in to Lynn, remember?"

"So?"

"So I wondered, did you meet her before she caught the bus? Or maybe, did you bump into her in Lynn?"

A tinge of red crept into his swarthy face. He rose slowly from the kitchen table. "All right, come on. Let's have it. What are you hinting at?"

She was a little frightened now, but she had gone too far to stop. "Don't you think I've seen the looks you've given her? How do I know you weren't seeing her on her day off? Or maybe right here when I wasn't around?"

"So that's it! I look at a babe and that means I'm sleeping with her. And when I get tired of her, I kill her. Is that what you're trying to say? And I suppose, like a good citizen, you're going to tell the cops."

"You know I wouldn't do that, Joe. I'm just thinking maybe somebody saw you, and if they did I could say like she was going on an errand for me, to cover you."

"I ought to break this over your face," he said, picking up the sugar bowl.

"Oh, yes? Well, don't you go acting innocent with me, Joe Serafino," she shouted. "Don't tell me you wouldn't make a pass at a girl living right here in the same house. I've seen you when you gave the girl and the kids a ride and how you'd brush up against her when you were helping her out of the car. How come you never have to help me out of the car? I saw you right here through the kitchen window. And how about the other girl, Gladys? Don't try to tell me there was nothing between you and her, with her walking around practically mother-naked in her room while you were sitting here in the kitchen and the door half open. And how many's the time—"

The doorbell rang. It was Hugh Lanigan.

"Mrs. Serafino? I want to ask you some questions."

11

ALICE HOSKINS, BRYN MAWR '57, THE MOTHER OF TWO CHIL-
dren and very obviously soon to have a third, invited the
chief of police into her living room. The floor was covered with an oyster-white wall-to-wall figured broad-
loom. The furniture was Danish modern, odd-shaped
pieces of highly polished teak and black sailcloth seemingly curved or sloping the wrong way, yet strangely
comfortable to sit in. There was a coffee table, a slab of
dark walnut supported by four glass legs. On one wall
hung a large abstract painting, vaguely suggestive of a
female head; on another, a grotesque ebony mask, the
features sharply etched and heightened in white. There
were ashtrays scattered about, of sharp-edged crystal,
most of them full to overflowing with cigarette butts. It
was the sort of room that could be attractive only if kept
scrupulously tidy with everything in its rightful place;
and the room was a mess. Toys were scattered about the
floor; a child's red sweater had been tossed on a chair of
wrought iron and white leather; a glass, a quarter full of
milk, was on the mantelpiece; a mussed newspaper was
on the couch.

Mrs. Hoskins, thin and drawn except for her protu-
berant belly, waddled over to the couch, swept the

newspaper onto the floor, and sat down. She patted the seat beside her in invitation, offered Lanigan a cigarette from a crystal box on the coffee table, and took one for herself. There was a matching table lighter, but as he reached for it she said, "It doesn't work," and struck a match for him.

"Celia is out with the children just now, but she should be back very soon," she said.

"It's just as well," he said. And then getting right to business: "Was she very friendly with Elspeth?"

"Celia is friendly with everybody, Mr. Lanigan. She's one of those plain girls who goes in for being friendly. You know, a plain girl has to have something else. Some go in for brains and some go in for causes and some go in for being friendly and good sports. That's Celia. She's jolly and a good sport and frightfully keen on the children. And they're crazy about her. I'm just here to have them; she takes care of them from then on."

"She been with you long?"

"Ever since before the first one arrived. She came to us when I was in my last month."

"So she's a good bit older than Elspeth?"

"Goodness, yes. Celia is twenty-eight or nine."

"Did she talk to you about Elspeth?"

"Oh yes. We talked about all kinds of things. We're quite good pals, you know. I mean, Celia has a lot of common sense even though she hasn't had much schooling. I think she left school about the second year of high, but she's been around and she knows people. She felt sorry for Elspeth. Celia is always feeling sorry for people. In this case, I suppose with some justification, Elspeth being a stranger and all. And the girl *was* shy. She didn't like to go places and do things. Celia bowls regularly and goes to dances and beach parties in the summer and skating in the winter, but she could never get Elspeth to come along. She would take in a movie with her occasionally, and of course they were together most afternoons with the children, but Celia could never get her to go bowling or to dances—you know, places where a girl could meet men."

"Surely you talked about the reason for it."

"Of course we did. Celia thought that part of it was

just natural shyness—some girls are, you know—and that maybe she didn't have the clothes for dances. Also, I suspect that Celia's crowd were probably too old for Elspeth."

Lanigan fished in his pocket and brought out a snapshot of the girl and the two Serafino children. "Mrs. Serafino gave me that. It was the only picture she had of the girl. Would you say it was a good likeness?"

"Oh, that's the girl all right."

"I mean, would you call that a characteristic expression, Mrs. Hoskins? We might run it in the papers—"

"You mean with the two children?"

"Oh no, we'd block them out."

"I suppose public curiosity must be satisfied, but I didn't realize the police were so cooperative," she said coldly.

He laughed. "It's the other way around, Mrs. Hoskins. We expect the press to cooperate by printing the picture. It may enable us to trace her movements yesterday."

"Oh, I'm sorry."

"And would you say that the expression is characteristic?" he persisted.

She looked at the snapshot again. "Yes, that's like her. She was really quite an attractive girl. A little on the stocky side, but not fat—what we used to call cornfed. Perhaps buxom would be a nicer word. Of course, I used to see her around with the children with little or no makeup and her hair just pulled back—but what woman does look nice when she's doing housework or taking care of children? I saw her all dressed up once in high heels and a party dress and her hair curled, and she looked quite lovely. It was just a few days after she came to work for the Serafinos. Oh, I remember—it was in February, Washington's Birthday. We'd bought a couple of tickets to the Policemen and Firemen's Ball. We gave them to Celia, of course—"

"Of course," murmured Lanigan.

"Well—" She hesitated and then blushed. "Oh, I'm sorry," she said.

"Don't apologize, Mrs. Hoskins. Everyone gives them away—usually to the maid."

85

"Well," she went on, "what I meant to say was that it was just like Celia to invite her instead of one of her men friends. Elspeth came over here because my husband was going to drive them down."

There was a noise at the front door and Mrs. Hoskins said, "That's Celia with the children now."

The door did not open so much as explode inward, and a moment later Hugh Lanigan found himself in the vortex of two children, Mrs. Hoskins, and the tall, plain Celia. The two women tried to divest the children of their sweaters and caps.

"I'll give them their lunch, Celia," said Mrs. Hoskins, "so that you can talk to this gentleman. He's here about poor Elspeth."

"I'm Chief Lanigan of the Barnard's Crossing police department," he began when they were alone in the living room.

"Yes, I know. I saw you at the Policemen and Firemen's Ball last Washington's Birthday. You led the Grand March with your missus. She's a looker."

"Thank you."

"And she looks smart too. I mean you can see that she's got something upstairs."

"Upstairs? Oh yes, I see. You're quite right. I can see that you're quite a judge of character, Celia. Tell me, what were your impressions of Elspeth."

Celia appeared to give the matter some thought before answering. "Well, most people thought of her as a quiet, mousy type, but you know that could have been just on the surface."

"How do you mean?"

"She was inclined to be stand-offish—not stuck-up, mind you, but sort of reserved. I figured the poor thing was all alone here and friendless, and I was sort of the old-timer in the neighborhood, so I decided it was my duty to kind of bring her out of her shell. Well, I had these two tickets to the Policemen and Firemen's Ball that Mr. Hoskins gave me. So I invited her, and she went and had a very nice time. She danced every dance, and during the intermission she had a fellow with her."

"And she was happy?"

"Well, she wasn't laughing and giggling all night, but

you could see she was having a good time in the quiet sort of way that was her style."

"That was a promising beginning."

"That was the end, too. I invited her to any number of dances and double dates after that but she never accepted. I've got lots of gentlemen friends and I could have fixed her up practically every Thursday night, but she always refused."

"Did you ever ask her why?"

"Of course I did, but she'd always say she just didn't feel like it, or she was tired and she wanted to get home early, or she had a headache."

"Perhaps she wasn't well," Lanigan suggested.

Celia shook her head. "Nothing like that. No girl ever gave up a date for a headache. I used to think maybe she didn't have the clothes, and being shy, you know, but then I thought maybe there was another reason." She lowered her voice. "I was waiting in her room once when we were going to a movie together. She was just getting dressed, and I was sort of looking at the things on her bureau while she was fixing her hair, and she had this sort of fancy box like a jewel box with a lot of pins and beads and hairpins, things like that in it. And I was just poking through, looking at her things—not nosy, you understand, but just looking—and I saw this wedding ring in the box. So I said, 'El, you getting ready to get married one of these days?' You know, sort of joking. Well, she got kind of red and closed the box and said something about it being her mother's."

"You think she may have been secretly married?"

"That would explain her not going out with fellows, wouldn't it?"

"Yes, it might. What did Mrs. Hoskins think about it?"

"I didn't tell her. I figured it was El's secret. If I told Mrs. Hoskins, she might mention it to someone and it might get back to the Serafinos and then Elspeth could lose her job. Not that that would have been such a bad idea, and many a time I've told her she ought to get another place."

"Didn't Mrs. Serafino treat her well?"

"I guess she treated her all right. Of course, they

weren't pals the way I am with Mrs. Hoskins, but you can't expect that. What bothered me was her having to be in that house all alone night after night with just the kids, and her room right on the first floor."

"She was frightened?"

"I know she was at first, and later I suppose she got used to it. This is a nice, quiet neighborhood and I guess after a while she felt safe enough."

"I see. Now about yesterday. Did you know what her plans were?"

Celia shook her head slowly. "I didn't see her all week, not since Tuesday when we took the children out for a walk." Her face brightened. "She said something then about not feeling well and thinking she might make an appointment with a doctor for a check-up. Then she said she might go to a movie. Come to think of it, she said something about going to the Elysium and I said it was an awfully long picture, and she said she could still make the last bus home and didn't mind walking from the bus stop that late—and here just what I was afraid of and warned her against happens." The tears came to Celia's eyes and she dabbed at them with her handkerchief.

The children had returned and stood looking wide-eyed at the two adults. When Celia began to cry, one of them ran up to hug her and the other began punching Lanigan with a tiny fist.

He reached down to hold the child away. "Take it easy, boy," he said, laughing.

Mrs. Hoskins appeared in the doorway. "He thinks you made Celia cry? Isn't that precious? Come here, Stephen. Come to mother."

It took some minutes before the children were mollified and once again led from the room. "Now Celia," said Lanigan when they were alone again, "what was it you were afraid of and what did you warn her against?"

Celia looked at him blankly and then she remembered. "Why, of going home late at night alone. I told her I wouldn't do it. It's so dark, that couple of blocks from the bus stop with the trees and all."

"But wasn't there anything in particular?"

"Well, I think that's something particular.

Again tears came to her eyes. "She was young and real innocent, The girl they had before her, Gladys, wasn't much older than she was, but I was never really friendly with her, for all that we went to a lot of places together. She was a wise kid who knew all the answers, but Elspeth . . ." She left it hanging there and then impulsively, "Tell me, was she all right when they found her? I mean, had she been, you know—mauled? I heard she was all naked when they found her."

He shook his head. "No. There was no sign that she had been sexually attacked. And she was decently dressed."

"I'm glad you told me," she said simply.

"It will be in the evening papers anyway." He got up. "You've been very helpful and I'm sure that if you think of something else, you'll let us know."

"I will, I will," she said and impulsively held out her hand. Lanigan took it and was mildly surprised to find she had the firm grip of a man. He started for the door, and then stopped as though a sudden thought had just occurred to him. "By the way, how did Mr. Serafino treat Elspeth? Was he decent to her?"

She gave him a look of approval, even admiration. "Now you're talking."

"Yes?"

She nodded. "He liked her. He let on that he didn't know she was alive, he hardly ever talked to her, but he was always watching her when he didn't think anyone was noticing. He's the kind that undresses a girl when he looks at her. That's what Gladys used to say, but she thought it was funny and kind of led him on."

"And what happened to her?"

"Oh, Mrs. Serafino got jealous and gave her the sack. I say when a wife is jealous, she usually has reason."

"I should think she would have hired an older woman then."

"And where would she get an older woman to take a job like that, six days a week and baby-sitting until two and three every morning?"

"I see your point."

"Besides, don't you think he had something to do with who got hired?"

12

LIEUTENANT EBAN JENNINGS OF THE BARNARD'S CROSSING
police force was an angular man in his late fifties with
watery blue eyes, and he dabbed at them constantly
with a handkerchief.

"Damn eyes start tearing first week in June and keep
on clear through September," he remarked as Hugh
Lanigan entered the office at the station house.

"Probably an allergy, Eban. You ought to get yourself
tested."

"I went through that a couple of years back. They
found I was sensitive to a lot of things, but none of them
that would hit just at this time. I figure maybe I'm
sensitive to summer residents."

"Could be, but they don't usually show up till the end
of June."

"Yes, but there's the anticipation. Get anything on
the girl?"

Lanigan tossed the snapshot that Mrs. Serafino had
given him onto the desk. "We'll give that to the papers.
Might start something."

Jennings examined the picture carefully. "She wasn't
bad-looking—sure a lot prettier than when I saw her this
morning. I like them built that way, kind of stocky. I

don't much care for these skinny little dames you see nowadays. I like a girl to be well-cushioned, know what I mean?"

"I know what you mean, Eban."

"And now I've got something for you, Hugh. The medical examiner's report came in." He handed his chief a paper. "Take a look at that last paragraph."

Lanigan emitted a low whistle. "The girl was two months pregnant."

"Yep, how do you like that? Somebody upstumped our little girl."

"It sort of gives a new slant to things, doesn't it? The people who knew her, Mrs. Serafino and her friend Celia and Mrs. Hoskins, are all agreed that she was quite shy and had no men friends at all."

Just then a patrolman walked by the door and he called him in. "Want to see you for a couple of minutes, Bill."

"Yes, sir." Patrolman William Norman was a young man with dark hair and a serious, businesslike demeanor. Although he had known Hugh Lanigan all his life and they had been on a first-name basis, characteristically he stood at attention and addressed the chief formally.

"Sit down, Bill."

Norman took one of the office chairs, managing to give the impression that he was still at attention.

"Sorry I couldn't let you off last night, but I had no one to cover for you. A man shouldn't have to work the night of his engagement party."

"Oh, that's all right, sir. Alice understood."

"She's a wonderful girl, and she'll make a fine wife. And the Ramsays are fine people."

"Yes, sir, thank you."

"I grew up with Bud Ramsay and I can remember Peggy in pigtails. They're conservative and kind of straitlaced, but the salt of the earth. And I tell you they didn't object to your taking your regular tour of duty—quite the contrary."

"Alice told me the party broke up a little after, so I guess I didn't miss much. I guess the Ramsays aren't much for staying up late anyway." He blushed slightly.

Lanigan turned to his desk to consult the duty roster. "Let's see, you came on duty last night at eleven?"

"Yes sir. I left the Ramsays at half-past ten in order to change into my uniform. The cruising car picked me up and dropped me off at Elm Square at a couple of minutes before eleven."

"You were headed up Maple Street to Vine?"

"Yes sir."

"You were supposed to pull the box on Vine Street at 1:00 A.M."

"Yes sir, I did." He reached into his high pocket and drew out a small notebook. "At one-three I pulled the box."

"Anything unusual from Maple to Vine?"

"No sir."

"On your route, did you meet anyone?"

"Meet someone?"

"Yes, did you see anyone walking down Maple as you were walking up?"

"No sir."

"Do you know Rabbi Small?"

"He was pointed out to me once and I've seen him around."

"Didn't you see him last night? He said he met you as he was walking home from the temple. That would be sometime after half-past twelve."

"No sir. From the time I finished trying doors in the Gordon block—that would be around a quarter-past twelve—to the time I rang in, I saw no one."

"That's curious. The rabbi says he saw you and you said good evening."

"No sir, not last night. I saw him coming home late from the temple a couple of nights ago and I spoke, but not last night."

"All right, what did you do when you got to the temple?"

"I tried the door to see that it was locked. There was a car in the parking lot and I flashed my light on it. Then I pulled the box."

"And you saw nothing unusual, or heard nothing unusual."

"No sir, just the car in the parking lot, and that wasn't too unusual."

"O.K., Bill. Thanks." Lanigan dismissed him.

"The rabbi told you he had seen Bill?" asked Jennings after Norman had left.

Lanigan nodded.

"So he was fibbing. What's it mean, Hugh? Think he could have done it?"

Lanigan shook his head slowly. "A rabbi? Not too likely."

"Why not? He lied about seeing Bill. That means he wasn't where he said he was, which means he could have been where he shouldn't have been."

"Why would he lie about something we could check on so easily? It doesn't make sense. More likely he was a little confused. He's a scholar. His head's in his books most of the time. You know, the president of the temple was at his house visiting when Stanley came to tell him some books he'd been expecting had arrived. So what does he do but run right out to the temple to look them over and stays in his study poring over them until well after midnight. A man like that, he could be a little confused about a casual meeting with a policeman a couple of days earlier. He could have telescoped the two nights and thought it was last night. Then it was actually a week ago."

"It seems to me his leaving a guest, especially where the guest is the president of the congregation, is pretty strange by itself. He says he was studying all night. Well, how do we know that he didn't meet the girl up there in his study? Look at the evidence, Hugh. The medical examiner fixes the time of the girl's death at one o'clock. Figure twenty minutes either way. The rabbi admits he was there about that time."

"No, twenty minutes to one is about the time he estimated he got home."

"But suppose he's shading the time a little, even five or ten minutes. Nobody saw him. The girl's handbag was in his car. And one thing more—" Jennings held up a forefinger—"today he didn't go to the services they hold every morning. How come? Was it because he didn't want to be around when the body was discovered?"

"Good Lord, the man is a rabbi, a religious man—"

"So what? He's a man, isn't he? How about that priest over in Salem a couple of years back? Father Damatopoulos? Didn't he get in trouble with a girl?"

Lanigan looked disgusted. "That was an entirely different case. He wasn't fooling around with the girl, in the first place. And in the second place, he's a Greek priest, and they're allowed to marry. They're even expected to, I understand. The trouble was that her folks tried to force a match."

"Well, I don't remember the details," Eban insisted doggedly, "but I remember there was some scandal connected with it."

"The only scandal was that a lot of people assumed that as a priest he wasn't supposed to marry, like the Roman Catholic priests. They thought it was terrible that a priest should be courting a girl. But the point is that as a Greek Orthodox priest, he had every right to."

"My point is that woman trouble can happen to any man," said Jennings. "That's the one thing, to my way of thinking, that his calling wouldn't protect him against. Any other crime in the book, stealing, breaking and entering, forging, assault, you could say a man who was a priest or a minister or a rabbi wouldn't do things like that. They wouldn't care enough about money, or they'd have better control of their tempers, but a woman can happen to any man, even a Roman priest. That's my way of looking at it."

"You've got a point there, Eban."

"And another thing, if not the rabbi, who've you got?"

"As to that, we've just started. But even then if you want to consider possibles there are plenty of them. Take Stanley. He's got a key to the temple. He's got a cot down in the basement. And the wall above the cot is covered with pictures of naked girls."

"He's a horny bastard, Stanley is," Eban agreed.

"And how about the job of carrying her to where she was finally dumped? That girl was no lightweight and the rabbi is not a big man. But that wouldn't faze Stanley."

"Uh-huh, but would he then go and put the girl's pocketbook in the rabbi's car?"

"He might. Or they could have been sitting there to get out of the rain. That jalopy he drives has no top to it. Yes, and another thing, suppose the man who murdered the girl had been carrying on with her for some little time, long enough to get her pregnant. Now between the two—the rabbi and the girl in his study, or Stanley and the girl in the basement—which is the more likely to be found out? If the rabbi had been meeting the girl, I'll bet Stanley would have known it inside of a week, especially since he cleans up every morning. Whereas if it were Stanley, the rabbi wouldn't find it out in a year."

"You've got a point there. What did Stanley tell you when you questioned him?"

Lanigan shrugged. "He claims he had a few beers at the Ship's Cabin and then went home. He's living at Mama Schofield's, but he says no one saw him come in. He could have met the girl after he left the Ship's Cabin and no one the wiser."

"It's the same story he gave me," said Jennings. "Why don't we pull him in and ask him a few questions?"

"Because we don't have a damn thing on him. You asked who it could be if not the rabbi, so I gave him as a possible. I'll give you another. How about Joe Serafino? He could have been carrying on with the girl right there in his own house. Mrs. Serafino did the shopping and ran the household. The girl was only a baby-sitter. All right, that means there must have been plenty of times when the missus was out of the house and Joe could have been with the girl. If his wife came home unexpectedly, why there was a bolt on the girl's door. Mrs. Serafino couldn't get in through the kitchen, and Joe could go out quietly through the back way. It could explain why the girl didn't have any boyfriends. She wouldn't need any if she had one right in the house where she lived. What's more, it could explain the way the girl was dressed when we found her. She must have come home, because she took her dress off and it was hanging in the closet. Suppose Joe came into her room just after and persuaded her to go out for a short walk. Since it was raining and she'd be wearing a coat anyway, she wouldn't go to the trouble of putting her dress on again. Besides, if they were that cozy he'd seen her in a lot less than a slip. Mrs. Serafino would be asleep and wouldn't know a thing about it."

"Now that has real possibilities, Hugh," declared Eban enthusiastically. "They could have gone for a walk and got as far as the temple when it really began to come down. Only natural that they'd take shelter in the rabbi's car."

"What's more, both Stanley and Celia, who was Elspeth's particular pal, hinted at some connection between Serafino and the girl. And I got the feeling that Mrs. Serafino was a little afraid her husband might be connected with the case. It's too bad I didn't get a chance to see him first thing in the morning."

"I did. We got him out of bed to identify the body. He was upset, but nothing more than you'd expect under the circumstances."

"What kind of car does he drive?"

"Buick convertible."

"I didn't see it."

"We might ask *him* a few questions," said Jennings.

Lanigan laughed. "And you'll find he was at that club of his from about eight o'clock Thursday evening to two o'clock Friday morning, and probably in plain sight of half a dozen employees and several dozen diners all the time. What I'm trying to tell you, Eban, is that if you're going to consider who could possibly have done it, there's no limit to the number of suspects. Here's another one: Celia. She was supposed to be the only one the dead girl knew. She's a big, strong, strapping young woman."

"You're forgetting that Elspeth was knocked up. Celia couldn't have done that no matter how big and strong and strapping she is."

"No I'm not. You're assuming the one responsible for her pregnancy is the one who killed her. It doesn't necessarily follow. Suppose Celia was in love with some man and Elspeth beat her time with him. Suppose he was responsible for the girl's pregnancy and suppose Celia found out. She admitted to me that she knew Elspeth had said something about going to a doctor for a check-up. Well, suppose she suspected what was really wrong, or suppose Elspeth confided in her. That would be only natural since she was all alone here. She'd want to confide in an older woman, and that could be only Celia. She might even tell her who was responsible, not knowing how Celia felt about the same man."

"But Elspeth didn't know any men."

"That's Celia's story. Mrs. Serafino didn't think she knew any man, but did mention something about some letters Elspeth got regularly, postmarked in Canada. I might also point out that Celia was away for the evening and probably got home late. Mrs. Hoskins would be asleep so she wouldn't know what time Celia got in. Suppose Celia noticed a light in Elspeth's room. She knew the girl had been to see the doctor, so she drops in to find out what happened. The girl had just had her fears confirmed and she wants to talk to someone about it. Celia persuades her to toss a coat on—her attire makes sense if she's with a girlfriend—and they go for a walk. It's raining quite hard by the time they come to the temple, so they get in the rabbi's car. It's then that Elspeth tells her who the man is and Celia, in a rage, chokes her."

"Any more?"

Hugh smiled. "That'll do for a starter."

"I'm still voting for the rabbi," said Eban.

Immediately after Lanigan left, the rabbi went to the temple. He did so out of a sense of fitness, not because he thought he could be of any help. There was nothing, unfortunately, he could do for the poor girl. And he was helpless when it came to police matters. Come to think of it, what more could he do at the temple than he could at home? But since the temple was involved he felt he should be there.

From his study, he watched the police go about busily measuring and photographing and searching. A group of idlers, some women but mostly men, followed the policemen about the parking lot, edging up close whenever they spoke. He wondered how so many managed to be free at that hour, but then he saw that the crowd was constantly changing. A man would stop his car and inquire what happened. When someone told him, he would join the group for a while and then leave. The crowd never varied very much in size.

There was actually little to see, but the rabbi could not tear himself away from the window. He had the venetian blind drawn and adjusted the slats so that he could look out without himself being observed from the parking lot. A uniformed officer was standing guard over his car, telling anyone who came too close to move on. There were reporters and news photographers on the scene now, and he wondered how long it would be before they discovered he was in his study and came up to interview him. He had no idea what to say to them, or whether he ought to talk to them at all. Perhaps the best thing would be to refer them to Mr. Wasserman, who would probably in turn refer them to the attorney who handled the temple legal affairs. But then, would not his refusal to discuss the case be regarded as suspicious?

The knock on the door, when it came, turned out to be not the reporters but the police. A tall, watery-eyed man introduced himself as Lieutenant Jennings. "Stanley told me you were here," he said.

The rabbi motioned him to a seat.

"We'd like to take your car down to the police garage, rabbi. We want to give it a good going-over and we can do it better down there."

"Certainly, lieutenant."

"You got a lawyer representing you, rabbi?"

The rabbi shook his head. "Should I have?"

"Well, maybe I shouldn't be the one to tell you, but we like to do things friendly-like. Maybe if you had a lawyer, he might tell you that you don't have to agree if you don't want to. Of course, if you didn't, we'd get a court order easy enough—"

"It's quite all right, lieutenant. If you think that taking my car downtown will help you in this shocking business, go right ahead."

"If you got your keys handy . . ."

"Of course." The rabbi detached them from the ring that was still lying on the desk. "This one is for the ignition and glove compartment, and this one is for the trunk."

"I'll give you a receipt for the car."

"It's not necessary."

He watched from the window as the lieutenant got into his car and drove off, and was pleased to see a good portion of the crowd leave with him.

Several times during the course of the day the rabbi tried to call his wife, but each time the line was reported busy. He called Mr. Wasserman's office, but was told that he was away and was not expected back.

He opened one of the books on his desk to leaf through it. Presently he made a note on a card. He checked a passage in another book and made another note. Soon he was completely absorbed in his research.

The phone rang. It was Miriam.

"I tried to get you three or four times, but the line was busy," he said.

"I took the receiver off the hook," she explained. "It started just after you left, people calling to ask if we had heard the news, and wanting to know if there was anything they could do. There was even one call to tell me that you had been arrested. That was when I took the receiver off, but then it makes funny little scratchy noises and you start wondering if it might be an important call. Didn't anyone call you?"

"Not a single call." He chuckled. "Guess no one wants to admit he's on speaking terms with Barnard's Crossing's Public Enemy Number One."

"Please don't! It's nothing to joke about." Then: "What are we going to do, David?"

"Do? Why, what is there to do?"

"I thought, what with all this—well, Mrs. Wasserman called up and invited us to stay with them—"

"But that's silly, Miriam. Tonight is the Sabbath and I intend to welcome it in my own house and at my own table. Don't worry, it will be all right. I'll be home in time for dinner, and then we'll go to the services as always."

"And what are you doing now?"

"Why I'm working on my Maimonides paper."

"Do you have to do that now?"

He wondered at the edge in her voice. "What else would I do?" he asked simply.

13

THERE WERE FOUR OR FIVE TIMES AS MANY PEOPLE AT EVEning services than as usual, much to the consternation of the members of Sisterhood, who had prepared cake and tea for the collation in the vestry afterward.

Considering the reason for the unexpectedly large attendance, the rabbi was none too pleased. He sat on the platform beside the Holy Ark, and grimly made up his mind that he would make no reference whatsoever to the tragedy. Pretending to be studying his prayer book, he glowered under his eyebrows at member after member who had never before attended a Friday evening service, smiling only when one of the few regulars entered, as if to show he knew they had come to worship rather than out of vulgar curiosity.

With Myra the president of Sisterhood, the Schwarzes were one of the regulars, but they usually sat fairly well back, in the sixth or seventh row. Tonight, however, although Ben slid into his regular seat, Myra continued on down front to the second row where the rabbi's wife was sitting. She sat down beside her, and leaning over, patted her hand and murmured in her ear. Miriam stiffened—then managed a smile.

The rabbi caught the little byplay and was touched by

this consideration on the part of the Sisterhood president, all the more because it was unexpected. But as he thought about it, its full significance began to dawn on him. It was a gesture of reassurance, the sympathy one extends to the wife of someone who is under suspicion. It gave him another explanation for the large attendance. Although some may have come in hopes he might speak of the crime, others wanted to see if he would show signs of guilt. To remain silent and not mention the affair might give the wrong impression and imply he was afraid to speak.

He made no mention of the subject in the course of his sermon, but later, near the close of the service, he said: "Before the mourners in the congregation rise to recite the Kaddish, I should like to recall to you the true significance of the prayer."

The congregation sat up and edged forward in their seats. Now he was coming to it.

"There is a belief," the rabbi went on, "that reciting the Kaddish is a duty the mourner owes to the dear departed. If you will read the prayer, or its English translation on the opposite page, you will notice that it contains no mention of death or any suggestion of a plea for the soul of the dead. Rather, it is an affirmation of the belief in God and in His power and glory. What is the significance of the prayer then? Why is it especially reserved for those who mourn? And why, when most of our prayers are whispered, is this one prayer said aloud?

"Perhaps our very manner of delivery will give a clue to its meaning. It is a prayer not for the dead but for the living. It is an open declaration by one who has just suffered the loss of a dear one that he still has faith in God. Nevertheless, our people persist in thinking of the Kaddish as an obligation they owe to the dead, and because in our tradition custom takes on the force of law, I shall recite the Kaddish with the mourners, for one who was not a member of this congregation, nor even of our faith, someone about whom we know little, but whose life happened through tragic accident to touch this congregation . . . .''

The rabbi and his wife said little as they walked home from the temple. Finally he broke the silence. "I noticed

101

Mrs. Schwarz went out of her way to extend her sympathy to you."

She s a good soul, David, and she meant well." Then, "Oh, David, this can be a nasty business."

"I'm beginning to think so," he said.

As they approached their house, they could hear the telephone ringing inside.

14

THE RELIGIOUS REVIVAL DID NOT EXTEND TO THE SATURDAY morning service; no more than the usual twenty or so turned up. When the rabbi got home, he found Chief Lanigan waiting for him.

"I don't like to intrude on your Sabbath," the chief apologized, "but neither do we like to interrupt our investigations. We police have no holidays."

"It's perfectly all right. In our religion, emergencies always supersede ritual."

"We're about through with your car. I'll have one of the boys drive it up here sometime tomorrow. Or if you're downtown, you can pick it up yourself."

"Fine."

"I'd like to check over with you what we found." From his briefcase he drew several pliofilm bags, each marked in black ink. "Let's see, this first one is stuff found under the front seat." He dumped the contents onto the desk. It consisted of some loose change, a receipt for repairs to the car dated several months back, a wrapper from a five-cent candy bar, a small calendar giving Hebrew and English equivalent dates, and a woman's plastic barrette.

The rabbi gave them a cursory glance. "Those are

ours. At least, I recognize the barrette as my wife's. But you can ask her to be sure."

"We already have," said Lanigan.

"I can't vouch for the candy wrapper or the money, but I have eaten that candy. It's kosher. That calendar is the kind that various institutions and business houses distribute on the Jewish New Year. I must get dozens of them each year." He opened his desk drawer. "Here's another."

"All right." Lanigan replaced the contents of the bag and emptied another on the desk. "This is the contents of the trash bag under the dashboard." There were several crumpled tissues with lipstick, a stick from a chocolate-covered Eskimo Pie, and an empty, crumpled cigarette package.

"Those look all right," said the rabbi.

"Does that look like your wife's lipstick?"

The rabbi smiled. "Why don't you check with her?"

"We have," said Lanigan, "and it is." He then offered the contents of the next bag, which was from the glove compartment. There was a crushed box of tissues, a lipstick, several road maps, a prayer book, a pencil, a plastic ball-point pen, half a dozen three-by-five cards, a two-cell flashlight, and a rumpled pack of cigarettes.

"That seems right," said the rabbi. "I think I can even be sure of the lipstick, because I remember when my wife got it I made some remark about its being worth a king's ransom if all that jewelry were real. I think my wife paid a dollar or a dollar and a half, and yet see with what brilliant gems it is encrusted."

"They sell thousands of them, so you would have no way of knowing if this particular one is your wife's."

"No, but surely it would be quite a coincidence if it were not."

"Coincidences happen, rabbi. The girl used the same lipstick. And it isn't such a terribly remarkable coincidence at that, since I gather it's a very popular make and a very popular shade for blondes."

"She was blonde then?"

"Yes, she was blonde. The flashlight, rabbi, shows no fingerprints."

The rabbi thought a moment. "The last time I recall

104

using it was to check the lipstick, after which I wiped it, of course."

"All that's left now is the contents of the ashtrays. The one in the rear had one cigarette, lipstick-stained. There were ten butts in the front ashtray, all the same brand and all lipstick-stained. Your wife's, I take it. You don't smoke."

"If I did, I don't think my cigarette would be lipstick-stained."

"Then that's about it. We're keeping these things for a while."

"Take all the time you need. How is the investigation going?"

"Well, we know quite a bit more than we did when I saw you yesterday. The medical examiner found no signs that she had been sexually attacked, but he did come up with one curious finding: the girl was pregnant."

"Could she have been married?"

"We don't even know that for sure. We found no marriage certificate among her effects at home, but in her purse, the one we found in your car, there was a wedding ring. Mrs. Serafino assumed that she was single, but if the girl had been secretly married, she never would have confided in her employer because it might have meant her job."

"Then that could account for her having the ring in her handbag instead of on her finger," suggested the rabbi. "She would wear it while she was with her husband and then take it off before coming home."

"That's a possibility."

"And have you arrived at any theory as to how the girl's handbag got in my car?"

"It could have been put there by the murderer deliberately to cast suspicion on you. Do you know anyone who might want to do that to you, rabbi?"

The rabbi shook his head. "There are a number of people in my congregation who don't care for me, but none who dislike me so much they would want to see me mixed up in this sort of thing. And I know almost no one here outside of the members of my congregation."

"No, it doesn't seem too likely, does it? But if someone didn't put it there, it can only mean the girl was in your car at some time. Then for some reason—perhaps the murderer had noticed the light in your study—she was transferred to where we found her."

"I suppose so."

Lanigan grinned. "There is another theory, rabbi, which we're duty-bound to consider because it fits the facts as we know them."

"I think I know. It is that when Stanley came to tell me my books had arrived I used that as an excuse to get out of the house in order to meet this girl. We had been having an affair and our meeting place was my study. I waited for her until I got tired or decided she was not going to appear, but she turned up just as the study door locked behind me. So we sat in my car and it was there she told me she was pregnant and that she expected me to divorce my wife and marry her to give her baby a name. So I strangled her and carried her body over to the grass plot beyond the wall. Then I coolly strolled home."

"It does sound silly, rabbi, but it's also possible as far as time and place are concerned. If I were asked to make book on it, I'd put it at a million to one. Nevertheless, if you told me you were planning a long trip someplace I'd have to tell you I'd rather you didn't."

"I understand," said the rabbi.

Lanigan opened the door to leave, then stopped. "Oh, there's another thing, rabbi. Patrolman Norman has no recollection of meeting you or anyone else that night." He grinned at the look of astonishment on the rabbi's face.

15

ELSPETH BLEECH'S PICTURE APPEARED IN THE SATURDAY papers, and by six that evening Hugh Lanigan was getting results. Nor was he altogether surprised. The girl had left the Serafino household early in the afternoon and had been gone all day. Surely a number of people must have seen her. Some would call almost immediately, but some might want to think over getting involved with the police.

The first call was from a doctor in Lynn who said he believed he had seen the young woman in question Thursday afternoon under the name of Mrs. Elizabeth Brown. She had given an address and telephone number. The street was the Serafinos', but the house number was reversed. The telephone number was that of the Hoskins.

The doctor reported that he had examined her and found her in excellent health and in the first stages of pregnancy. Had she appeared upset or nervous? No more than many of his patients in similar circumstances. Many were delighted when they discovered they were pregnant, but there were also any number who found the news upsetting, even though they were legitimately married.

Had she mentioned her plans for the rest of the afternoon or evening? He was sure she had not. Perhaps she had spoken to his secretary, who had now already left for the day. If the police thought it important he would get in touch with her and inquire. They did, and he said he would.

Almost immediately there came another call, this time from the secretary, who had seen the girl's picture in the paper and was sure she had been in the office Thursday afternoon. No, she had noticed nothing unusual. No, the girl had not mentioned what her plans were for the afternoon or evening. Oh yes, just before leaving, she had asked where she could make a call. The secretary had offered the office phone, but she preferred the privacy of a pay station.

Then came a rash of telephone calls from people who were sure they had seen her, some in stores in Lynn, where she could have been, and others from nearby towns, where the likelihood was less. A gasoline station attendant called in to say she had been on the back seat of a motorcycle that had stopped for directions. There was even a call from an operator of an amusement park in New Hampshire who insisted the girl had been there around three o'clock to ask for a job in one of the concessions.

Lanigan remained at his desk until seven and then went home for his dinner, leaving strict orders that any call concerning Elspeth Bleech should be transferred to him at home. Fortunately, none came in and he was able to eat in peace. He had no sooner finished, however, than his doorbell rang; he opened the door to Mrs. Agnes Gresham, who owned and operated the Surfside Restaurant.

Mrs. Gresham was a fine-looking woman of sixty with beautifully coiffed snow-white hair. She carried herself with the dignity becoming to one of the town's leading business-women.

"I called the police station and they told me you had gone home, Hugh." Her tone carried a faint air of disapproval.

"Come right in, Aggie. Can I get you a cup of coffee?"

108

"This is business," she said.

"There's no law that says we can't be comfortable while talking business. Can I fix you a drink?"

This time she refused more graciously, and took the seat he indicated.

"Okay, Aggie, is it my business or your business?"

"It's your business, Hugh Lanigan. That girl whose picture was in the paper—she was in my restaurant having dinner Thursday night."

"Around what time?"

"From before half-past seven when I took over the cashier's cage so that Mary Trumbull could get her dinner, to around eight o'clock."

"This for sure, Aggie?"

"I am quite sure. I took particular notice of the girl."

"Why?"

"Because of the man she was with."

"Oh? Can you describe him?"

"He was about forty years old, dark, good-looking. When they finished eating, they left the restaurant and got into a big blue Lincoln that was parked in front of the door."

"What made you pay such particular attention to him? Were they arguing or quarreling?"

She shook her head impatiently. "I noticed them because I knew him."

"Who was it?"

"I don't know his name, but I know where he works. I bought my car at the Becker Ford Agency and I saw him there once behind a desk when I went there on business."

"You've been very helpful, Aggie, and I appreciate it."

"I do my duty."

"I'm sure you do."

As soon as she was gone, he telephoned the Becker home.

"Mr. Becker is not in. This is Mrs. Becker. Can I help you?"

"Perhaps you can, Mrs. Becker." Lanigan introduced

109

himself. "Can you tell me the name of the person in your husband's employ who drives a blue Lincoln?"

"Well, my husband drives a black Lincoln."

"No, this is blue."

"Oh, you must mean my husband's partner, Melvin Bronstein. He has a blue Lincoln. Is anything wrong?"

"No, nothing at all, ma'am."

Then he called Lieutenant Jennings. "Any luck at the Serafinos'?"

"Not much, but I did get something. The Simpsons across the way saw a car parked in front of the Serafino house very late Thursday night, midnight or even later."

"A blue Lincoln?"

"How'd you know?"

"Never mind, Eban. Meet me at the station right away. We've got work to do."

Eban Jennings was already there when he arrived. Hugh filled him in on what Aggie Gresham had said. "Now Eban, I want a picture of this Melvin Bronstein. Go down to the offices of the *Lynn Examiner*."

"What makes you so sure they'll have one?"

"Because this Bronstein lives in Grove Point and owns a car agency. That makes him important, and anyone who's important gets put on a committee of some kind or is made an officer of some organization, and the first thing they do is have their picture taken and printed in the *Examiner*. Look through everything they have on him and get a nice clear picture that shows his features plainly and have about half a dozen of them printed up."

"We going to give these to the papers?"

"No. As soon as you have the prints, you and maybe Smith and Henderson—I'll look through the roster and line up a couple or three men—will drive along Routes 14, 69, and 119. You'll stop at every motel and show Bronstein's picture, and see if he's stayed there any time in the last few months. You can't go by their registers because chances are that he didn't sign under his right name."

"I don't get it."

"What don't you get? If you had a girl you wanted to shack up with, where would you take her?"

"Up in back of Chisholm's barn."

"Tcha. You'd drive up country and stop at a motel. That girl was pregnant. She may have got that way in the back seat of a car, but she also may have got that way in some motel not too far from here."

16

SUNDAY MORNING WAS BRIGHT AND SUNNY; THE SKY WAS cloudless and there was a gentle breeze off the water. It was perfect weather for golf, and as the board of directors of the temple dribbled in to the meeting room their clothes indicated that many of them would be off to the links the moment the meeting was adjourned.

Jacob Wasserman watched them come in by twos and threes and knew he was beaten. He knew it by the number who finally appeared, almost the full complement of forty-five. He knew it by the friendly way they greeted Al Becker and the way he was avoided by the few who had told him they were still undecided. He knew it by a sudden realization that the great majority were all the same type: sleek, successful professional men and businessmen who belonged to the temple primarily as a social obligation, who were used to and expected the best of everything, who could be expected to have the same attitude toward a casual, unfashionable rabbi as they might toward an inefficient junior executive in their employ. He saw all this in their ill-concealed impatience to get on with the unpleasant business at hand and go about their pleasures, and he blamed himself for having permitted so many men like this to be nominated for the board. He had yielded to the needs of the building committee, who had recommended each candidate on the grounds that he was doing all right for himself. "If we put him on the board, there's a good chance he'll kick in with a sizable contribution."

He called the meeting to order, and proceeded through the reading of minutes and the reports of committees. There was an audible sigh when Wasserman completed Old Business and began to explain the issues involved in the rabbi's contract. "Before I call for discussion," he concluded, "I should like to point out that Rabbi Small is willing to remain, although I imagine he could probably better himself by going elsewhere." (He knew no such thing, of course.) "I have been in closer touch with the rabbi than has anyone else in the congregation. That is only natural in my capacity as chairman of the ritual committee. I would like to say at this point that I am more than satisfied with the way he has carried on his duties.

"Most of you see the rabbi only in his public capacity, when he is conducting services on the holidays, or when he is addressing a meeting. But there is a great deal of work of a more private nature that is part of his job. Take weddings for example. One of the marriages this year involved a girl who was not Jewish. There were lengthy discussions with both sets of parents, and when the girl decided to accept Judaism the rabbi gave her a course of instruction in our religion. He meets with every one of the Bar Mitzvah boys individually. As chairman of the ritual committee, I can tell you that we go over every service together. He is in constant touch with the principal of the religious school. And then there are dozens—dozens? hundreds—of calls from outsiders, both from Jews and from Gentiles, from individuals and from organizations, some having nothing to do with the temple, all with questions, requests, plans, that have to be considered and discussed. I could go on all morning, but then you would never get to the golf course."

There was appreciative laughter.

"To most of you," he went on seriously, "these and countless other phases of the rabbi's work are unknown. But they are known to me. And I want to say that the rabbi has done his work even better than I had hoped when we first hired him."

Al Becker raised his hand and was recognized. "I'm not so sure that I care for the idea of the rabbi we employ and whose salary we pay, busying himself with matters that have no connection with this temple. But maybe our good president is stretching things a little." He leaned forward, and supporting himself on the table with his two clenched fists, looked around at each of the members and went on in a loud voice. "Now, there is no one here who has a greater respect for our president, Jake Wasserman, than I have. I respect him as a man, and I respect the work he has done for the temple. I respect his integrity and I respect his judgment. Normally, if he said to me, this fellow is a good man, I'd be willing to gamble that he was. And when he says that the rabbi is a good man, I'm sure he is." His jaw protruded aggressively. "But I say he is not a good man for this particular job. He may be an excellent rabbi, but not for this congregation. I understand he's a fine scholar, but right now that's not what we need. We are part of a community. In the eyes of our non-Jewish neighbors and friends we are one religious organization of the several in the community. We need someone who will represent us properly to our Gentile neighbors and friends. We need someone who can make an impressive appearance on a public platform, who can carry on the public relations job that the position requires. The headmaster of the high school confided in me that next year he plans to offer the honor of making the graduation address to the spiritual leader of our temple. Frankly, friends, the sight of our present rabbi up on the stage in baggy pants and unpressed jacket, his hair uncombed, his tie twisted, speaking as he usually does with little stories from the Talmud and his usual hair-splitting logic—well, frankly, I would be embarrassed."

Abe Reich was recognized. "I just want to say this: I know exactly what Mr. Wasserman means when he says the rabbi is involved in a lot of other activities that most of us don't realize. I myself had the privilege of seeing this side of the rabbi, and let me tell you it was an important matter to me and I have been full of admiration for the rabbi ever since. Maybe he's no Fourth of July orator, but when he talks to us from the pulpit, he talks sense and he reaches me. I'd rather have that than someone who puts on an act and uses a bunch of ten-dollar words. When he talks I feel he's sincere, and that's more than I can say about a lot of high-powered rabbis I've heard."

Dr. Pearlstein rose to support his friend, Al Becker. "A dozen times a week when I prescribe for a patient I am asked if they can use the same medicine I prescribed for them last year, or that I prescribed for someone they know who had the same symptoms. I have to explain that an ethical doctor prescribes for a particular person for a particular condition—"

"Nothing like getting a plug in, Doc," someone shouted, and the doctor joined in the laughter.

"What I mean to say is that it's like Al Becker said. No one claims that the rabbi is incapable or insincere. The question is, is he the rabbi that this congregation needs at this time? Is he what the doctor ordered for this particular patient in this particular condition?"

"Yeah, but maybe there's more than one doctor."

Several were shouting at the same time, and Wasserman banged on the desk for order.

One of those who had never attended a board meeting before raised his hand and was recognized. "Look fellows," he said, "what's the sense of our discussing this? When you talk about an idea or about some project, okay, so the more you talk, the clearer it gets. But when you talk about a person, you don't get anywhere. You just get a lot of bad feeling. Now all of us know the rabbi and we know whether we want him or not. I say, let's not discuss the matter any further and let's vote."

"That's right!"

"Move the previous question!"

"Let's vote."

"Just a minute." It was the roar that everyone recognized as belonging to Abe Casson, who had developed its raucousness and its volume at a thousand political meetings. "Before you move the previous question, I'd like to say a few words on the situation in general." He left his seat and walked down the aisle to the front of the room to face them. "I'm not going to argue whether the rabbi is doing a good job or not. But I am going to say a few words on public relations, which my good friend Al Becker has brought up. As you all know, when a Catholic priest is assigned to a parish by his bishop, he stays there until the bishop reassigns him. And if any member of the parish doesn't like him, he is free—to move out of the parish. It's different with the different Protestant churches. They all have different ways of hiring a minister and of dropping him, but in general, they don't fire a minister unless there's something definite that he's done, and it has to be something pretty God-awful definite."

He lowered his voice to a more conversational tone. "Now I've been chairman of the Republican committee of the county for almost ten years now, so I guess I can lay claim to knowing about the way our non-Jewish friends and neighbors think. They don't understand our method of engaging a rabbi or of firing him. They don't understand that twenty minutes after a rabbi lands in town, there's a pro-rabbi and an anti-rabbi party. They can't understand how some members of the congregation can become anti-rabbi just because they don't like the kind of hats his wife wears. It's routine with us. As a man in politics all my life, I know all the goings-on in all the temples and synagogues in Lynn and Salem, yes and in most of the Boston ones too. When a rabbi takes over a new pulpit, there is a group made up of friends of the last rabbi that is automatically opposed to him. That's the way it is with us Jews. Now the Gentiles don't understand this, as I say. So when we fire the rabbi the first thing they'll think is that there must have been some big reason. Now what reason is bound to occur to them? Let's think about it. Just a few days ago, a young girl was found murdered in our backyard. As you know, at the time our rabbi was alone in the temple, in his study. His car was in the parking lot, and the girl's handbag was found in his car. Now you and I know, and the police know too, that the rabbi could not have done it—"

"Why couldn't the rabbi have done it?" asked a member.

There was dead silence at this open expression of

what had not been entirely absent from the minds of many of them.

But Casson turned on them. "Whoever said that ought to be ashamed of himself. I know the men in this room and I'm sure that no one here really thinks the rabbi could have done this terrible thing. As the campaign manager of the present district attorney, I can tell you that I have some idea of what his thinking is and what the thinking of the police is. I tell you that they don't for a minute think that the rabbi did this. But"—he leveled a forefinger at them for emphasis—"he has to be considered. If he weren't a rabbi, he would be the A-number-one suspect." He held up his hand and ticked off on his fingers the points as he made them. "Her bag was found in his car. He was there at the time. He is the only one we know for sure was there. We have only his word that he was in his study all the time. There is no other suspect."

He looked around impressively. "And now, two days after the event you want to fire him. How's that for public relations, Al? What are your Gentile friends going to think when they find out that two days after the rabbi becomes a suspect in a murder case, his congregation fired him? What are you going to say to them, Al? 'Oh, we didn't fire him for that. We fired him because his pants weren't pressed.' "

Al Becker rose. He was no longer quite so sure of himself. "Look, I have nothing against the rabbi personally. I want that distinctly understood. I am only thinking of what is best for the temple. Now if I thought that what our friend Abe Casson just told us might turn the scales against the rabbi, that as a result of our firing him he might get mixed up in this murder—more mixed up than he is right now, that is—I'd say, no. But you know and I know that the police can't seriously connect him with this crime. You know that they're not going to try to pin it on him because we drop him. And if we don't, then we have him for all of next year."

"Just a minute, Al." It was Casson again. "I don't think you get the point. I'm not concerned with the reaction to the rabbi. I'm concerned with the reaction to the temple, to the congregation. Some are going to say that we dropped him because we suspected he was guilty. And they'll say we must have a fine bunch of men in the rabbinate if one of them could be so quickly suspected of murder. And there'll be others who'll think it absurd that the rabbi could be suspected. And all they'll think is that we Jews don't trust each other and are willing to fire our spiritual leader just on suspicion. In this country where a man is considered innocent until he's proved guilty, that won't sit so well. Do you get it, Al? It's us I'm concerned about."

"Well, I'm not voting another contract to the rabbi," said Becker, and sat back with arms folded as if to show he wanted no further part in the proceedings.

"What are we fighting for?" It was another member whom Becker had induced to come vote against the rabbi. "I can see Abe Casson's point of view, and I can see Al Becker's point of view. But I can't see why we have to make up our minds today. There's another meeting next week. The police work fast these days. By the next meeting the whole thing may be all settled. I say, let's lay the matter on the table until then. And if worst comes to worst, we can still have another meeting."

"If the worst comes, you won't have to bother about another meeting," said Abe Casson grimly.

17

WASSERMAN HAD BEEN SO SURE THE RABBI WOULD LOSE that his face could not help showing his relief.

"Believe me, rabbi," he said, "the future looks brighter. Who can tell what will happen in the next week or two? Suppose the police don't come up with the guilty man, then do you think we will permit another postponement? No, I'll put my foot down. I'll tell them that it isn't fair to you to keep you waiting this way when you could be looking for another position. I'm sure they'll see the justice of that. But even if thy police do find the man, do you think Al Becker will be able to rally the same number of people at the next meeting? Believe me, I know these people. I have tried to get them to come to meetings. Maybe he could turn the trick once, but he won't be able to a second tlme. And if we have the usual people present, I'm sure we'll win."

The rabbi was troubled. "I feel as if I'm forcing myself on them. Maybe what I ought to do is to resign. It's not pleasant to hold a pulpit on sufferance. It's not dignified."

"Rabbi, rabbi. We've got over three hundred members. If it came to a vote of the entire membership, believe me you'd get a majority. I tell you, the great majority of the membership is with you. These board members—it's not as if they were the representatives of the congregation. They were appointed. I appointed them, or at least I appointed the nominating committee that appointed the slate, and you know what happens—the membership endorse the slate as a whole. These board members, they're people that we hoped would do some work for the temple or they're people who are a little richer than the rest. But they represent only themselves. Becker reached them first so they voted his way. But if he asks them to come to the next meeting, he'll find that they all have previous appointments."

The rabbi laughed. "You know, Mr. Wasserman, at the seminary one of the favorite subjects of discussion in student bull sessions was what a rabbi could do to ensure his job. The best way is to marry a very rich girl. Then the congregation feels that it doesn't make any difference to you whether you stay or leave. This gives you a tremendous psychological advantage. Then too, if she is indeed very rich, that gives her social position in the congregation, and this counts for a great deal with the wives of the members. Another way is to write and publish a popular book. The congregation then takes on prestige vicariously. Their rabbi is a famous author. A third way is to get into local politics so that the Gentiles speak well of you. If you develop a reputation in the community of being a 'rabbi with guts,' it's practically impossible to fire you. But now I could offer still another way: become a suspect in a murder case. This is a fine way for a rabbi to ensure his position."

But the rabbi returned from seeing Wasserman to his car much less light-heartedly. He watched gloomily as Miriam went through her usual ministrations after Sunday dinner, arranging the fruit bowl on the coffee table in the living room, puffing up the cushions on the couch and the easy chairs, giving a last-minute dusting to the tables and the lamps.

"Expecting someone?" he asked.

"No one in particular, but people always drop in Sunday afternoon, especially when it's so nice out. Don't you think you had better put on your jacket?"

"Frankly, right now I'm a little fed up with my congregation and my pastoral duties. Do you realize, Miriam, that we've been here in Barnard's Crossing almost a year and we've never really explored the town? Let's take a holiday. Suppose you change into some comfortable shoes and we'll take a bus downtown and just wander around.''

"Doing what?"

"Nothing, I hope. If you feel we really need an excuse, we can stop at the police station and recover the car. But I would just like to meander like a tourist through the narrow, crooked streets of Old Town. It's a fascinating place, and has quite a history. Did you know that Barnard's Crossing was originally settled by a bunch of roughnecks, sailors and fishermen for the most part, who didn't care to live under the repression of the Puritan theocracy. Ever since Hugh Lanigan told me that I have done a little checking on my own. They didn't observe the Sabbath too carefully here, or even have a church or a minister for years after the place was settled. And we thought it was a staid, stuffy, ultra-conservative community. Barnard's Crossing breeds a special kind of independence that you don't find in the average New England town. Most New England towns have a tradition of independence, but all it means is that they took an active part in the Revolution. Here there is also a tradition of independence against the rest of New England. It's land's end, so they tend to be suspicious of the rest of the world. Why don't we look it over.''

They left the bus near the edge of Old Town and sauntered along, stopping whenever they saw anything of interest. They went into the town hall and gawked at the old battle flags that were mounted in glass cases along the walls. They read the bronze plaques that had been set up on the historic buildings. At one point they found themselves part of a crowd of sightseers who were being lectured by a guide, and they went along until the party returned to their bus. Then they walked along the main street looking at the windows of the antique shops, the gift shops, and the wonderful window of a ship chandler with its coils of rope, its brass ship fittings, compasses, and anchors. They found a little park that overlooked the harbor, and sat on one of the

121

benches and just looked down at the water with its boats, some sailing along gracefully, others, motor-powered, scooting along the surface like water bugs. They did not talk but just drank in the peaceful scene.

Finally they set out to find the police garage to re-claim their car, and promptly got lost. For an hour or so, they wandered in and out of little blind alleys with sidewalks so narrow two could not walk abreast. They were flanked on either side by frame houses, often less than a foot apart, but they looked down these narrow slits to see, in back, tiny old-fashioned gardens with rock flowers and hollyhocks and sunflowers and little arbors covered with vines. They retraced their steps and wandered into another little private street where the few houses were of painted brick and had gardens enclosed by white picket fences; beyond, they could glimpse the water with a boat bobbing up and down beside a rickety landing that lurched under every movement of the waves. Occasionally, they caught sight of someone in a bathing suit lying on the landing, taking the sun, and they quickly averted their eyes as though they were intruding; unconsciously they found themselves lowering their voices.

The sun was hot and they were beginning to grow tired. There was no one about to ask the way back to the main street. The front porches they passed usually were set back from the street and sealed off by the inevitable white picket fence. To push back the gate and walk up fifty feet of flagstone path and knock on the door of the screened-in porch seemed an invasion of privacy. The entire atmosphere seemed designed to keep one's neighbor at arm's length, not from unfriendliness but rather as though each householder were content to cultivate his own garden.

Then, quite suddenly, they found themselves on a street that skirted the waterfront, and a block ahead they saw the main street with its many shops. They quickened their pace to make sure they wouldn't lose sight of it again, but just as they were about to turn in, they were hailed by Hugh Lanigan, relaxing on his front porch.

"Come on up and sit for a while," he called. They needed no second invitation.

"I thought you'd be working," said the rabbi with a grin. "Or is the case solved?"

Lanigan smiled back. "Just taking a breather, rabbi—just like you. But I'm no further away from my work than the telephone."

It was a large, comfortable porch with wicker armchairs. No sooner were they seated than Mrs. Lanigan, a slim gray-haired woman in sweater and slacks, came out to join them.

"You can have a drink, can't you, rabbi?" asked Lanigan anxiously. "I mean, it's not against your religion?"

"No, we're not Prohibitionists. I take it you're offering me one like yours."

"Right, and no one makes a Tom Collins like Amy here."

"How is the investigation going?" the rabbi asked when Mrs. Lanigan had returned with a tray.

"We're making progress," said the chief cheerfully. "How is your congregation?"

"Making progress," said the rabbi with a smile.

"I understand you're having your troubles with them."

The rabbi looked at him questioningly, but said nothing.

Lanigan laughed. "Look, rabbi, let me teach you something about police work. In a big city there's what might be called a stable criminal population that accounts for most of the crime the police have to contend with. And how do they control it? Largely through informers. In a town like this, we don't have a criminal population. We do have a few chronic troublemakers, but the way we control the situation is the same way, through informers. Only they're not regular informers. It's just a lot of gossip that we hear, that we listen to carefully. I know what's happening in your temple almost as well as you. At the meeting today there were about forty people present. And when they got home, they all told their wives. Now do you think that eighty people can keep a secret in a town like this, especially when it's not supposed to be a secret in the first place? Ah, rabbi, we do these things so much better in our church. With us, what the priest says, goes."

"Is he so much a better man than the rest of you?" asked the rabbi.

"He's a good man usually," said Lanigan, "because the process of selection screens out most of the incompetents. Of course, we have some damn fools in the clergy, but that's not the point. The point is that if you're going to have discipline, you have to have someone whose authority is not subject to question."

"I suppose that's the difference between the two systems," said the rabbi. "We encourage the questioning of everything."

"Even matters of faith?"

"There is very little in the way of faith that is demanded of us. And that little, such as the existence of a single All-Powerful, All-Knowing, Ever-Present God, we do not forbid to be questioned. We merely recognize that it leads nowhere. But we have no articles of faith which must be subscribed to. For example, when I got my S'michah—you call it ordination—I was not questioned on my beliefs and I took no oath of any sort."

"You mean you are not dedicated in any way?"

"Only as I feel myself dedicated."

"Then what makes you different from the members of your flock?"

The rabbi laughed. "They are not my flock in the first place, at least not in the sense that they are in my care and that I am responsible to God for their safety and their behavior. Actually, I have no responsibility, or for that matter no privilege, that every male member of my congregation over the age of thirteen does not have. I presumably differ from the average member of my congregation only in that I am supposed to have a greater knowledge of the Law and of our tradition. That is all."

"But you lead them in prayer—" He stopped when he saw his guest shaking his head.

"Any adult male can do that. At our daily service it is customary to offer the honor of leading the prayers to any stranger who happens to come in, or to anyone who is not usually there."

"But you bless them and you visit the sick and you marry them and you bury them—"

"I marry them because the civil authorities have

empowered me to; I visit the sick because it is a blessing that is enjoined on everyone; I do it as a matter of routine, largely because of the example set by your priests and ministers. Even the blessing of the congregation is officially the function of those members of the congregation who happen to be descendants of Aaron, which is the custom in Orthodox congregations. In Conservative temples like ours, it is really a usurpation on the part of the rabbi."

"I see now what you mean when you say you are not a man of the cloth," said Lanigan slowly. Then a thought occurred to him. "But how do you keep your congregation in line?"

The rabbi smiled ruefully. "I don't seem to be doing a very good job of it, do I?"

"That's not what I meant. I wasn't thinking of your present difficulties. I mean, how do you keep them from sinning?"

"You mean how does the system work? I suppose by making everyone feel responsible for his own acts."

"Free will? We have that."

"Of course, but ours is a little different. You give your people free will, but you also give them a helping hand if their foot slips. You have a priest who can hear confession and forgive. You have a hierarchy of saints who can intercede for the sinner, and finally you have a Purgatory, which is in the nature of a second chance. I might add that you have a Heaven and a Hell that help to right any wrongs in life on this earth. Our people have only the one chance. Our good deeds must be done on this earth in this life. And since there is no one to share the burden with them or to intercede for them they must do it on their own."

"Don't you people believe in Heaven, or in life after death?"

"Not really," said the rabbi. "Our beliefs have been influenced by those around us, of course, as have yours. At times in our history concepts of a life after death have cropped up, but even then we saw them our own way. Life after death means for us that part of our life that lives on in our children, in the influence that survives us after death, and the memories people have of us."

"Then if someone is evil in this life, and yet is prosperous and happy and healthy, he gets away with it?" It was Mrs. Lanigan who asked the question.

The rabbi turned to face her. He wondered if her question had perhaps been prompted by some personal experience. "It's questionable," he said slowly, "whether a thinking organism like man can ever 'get away with' something he's done. Nevertheless, it is a problem, and all the religions have wrestled with it: how does the good man who suffers get recompense and the evil man who prospers get punished? The Eastern religions explain it by reincarnation. The wicked man who is prosperous merited his prosperity by his virtue in a previous reincarnation and his wickedness will be punished in his next reincarnation. The Christian church answers the question by offering Heaven and Hell." He appeared to consider, and then he nodded his head briskly. "They're both good solutions, if you can believe them. We can't. Our view is given in the Book of Job, which is why it is included in the Bible. Job is made to suffer undeservedly, but there is no suggestion that he will be recompensed in the next life. The suffering of the virtuous is one of the penalties of living. The fire burns the good man just as severely and painfully as it does the wicked."

"Then why bother to be good?" asked Mrs. Lanigan.

"Because virtue really does carry its own reward and evil its own punishment. Because evil is always essentially small and petty and mean and depraved, and in a limited life it represents a portion wasted, misused, and that can never be regained."

His tone while he was talking to Hugh Lanigan had been conversational and matter-of-fact, but as he spoke to Mrs. Lanigan it grew solemn and portentous, almost as though he were delivering a sermon. Miriam coughed warningly to him. "We should be getting back, David," she said.

The rabbi looked at his watch. "Why, it is getting late. I didn't meam to run on this way. I suspect it was the Tom Collins."

"I'm glad you did, rabbi," said Lanigan. "You might

not think it, but I'm very interested in religion. I read books on the subject whenever I can. I don't get a chance to discuss it very often though. People are reluctant to talk about religion."

"Maybe it's no longer very important to them," he suggested.

"Well, now, that might very well be, rabbi. But I enjoyed this afternoon, and I'd like to repeat it sometime."

The telephone rang. Mrs. Lanigan went inside to answer it and returned almost immediately. "It's Eban on the phone, Hugh."

Her husband, in the midst of explaining the shortest way to the police garage, said, "Tell him I'll call him back."

"He's not at home," she said. "He's calling from a pay station."

"Oh, all right, I'll talk to him."

"We'll find our way," said the rabbi. Lanigan nodded absently and hurried inside. As he walked down the porch steps, the rabbi was vaguely disturbed.

18

THE NEXT MORNING MELVIN BRONSTEIN WAS ARRESTED. Shortly after seven, while the Bronsteins were still at breakfast, Eban Jennings and a sergeant, both in plain clothes, appeared at the Bronstein home.

"Melvin Bronstein?" asked Jennings when a man answered the door.

"That's right."

The policeman showed his badge. "I'm Lieutenant Jennings of the Barnard's Crossing police department. I have a warrant for your arrest."

"What for?"

"You're wanted for questioning in the matter of the murder of Elspeth Bleech."

"Are you charging me with murder?"

"My instructions are to bring you in for questioning," said Jennings.

Mrs. Bronstein called from the dining room, "Who is it, Mel?"

"Just a minute, dear," he called back.

"You're going to have to tell her," said Jennings, not unkindly.

"Will you come with me?" Bronstein asked in a low voice, and led the way to the dining room.

Mrs. Bronstein looked up, startled.

"These gentlemen are from the police department, dear," he said. "They want me to come to the police station to give them some information and to answer some questions." He swallowed hard. "It's about that poor girl who was found in the temple yard."

A spot of color appeared in Mrs. Bronstein's naturally pale face, but she did not lose her composure. "Do you know anything about the girl's death, Mel?" she asked.

"Nothing about her death," said Bronstein with great earnestness, "but I know something about the girl and these gentlemen think it might help them in their investigation."

"Will you be home for lunch?" asked his wife.

Bronstein looked at the policemen for an answer.

Jennings cleared his throat. "I don't think I'd count on it, ma'am."

Mrs. Bronstein placed her hands against the edge of the table and gave a slight push. She rolled back a few inches, and the policemen realized for the first time that she was in a wheelchair.

"If you can be of any help to the police in their investigation of this terrible business, Mel, then of course you must do everything you can."

He nodded. "You better call Al and ask him to get in touch with Nate Greenspan."

"Of course."

"Do you want me to help you back to bed," he asked "or will you sit up?"

"I think I'd better go back to bed."

He bent down and scooped her up in his arms. For a moment he just stood there, holding her. She looked deep into his eyes.

"It's all right, sweetheart," he whispered.

"Of course," she murmured.

He carried her out of the room.

The news spread like wildfire. The rabbi had just returned from a busy morning at the temple and was about to sit down to lunch when Ben Schwarz called to tell him.

"Are you sure?" asked the rabbi.

129

"Oh, it's on the level, rabbi. It will probably be on the next radio news broadcast."

"Do you have any details?"

"No, just that he was taken into custody for questioning." He hesitated and then said, "Er—rabbi, I don't know how it will affect anything you might be planning to do, but I think you ought to know that he's not a member of our temple."

"I see. Well, thank you."

He reported the conversation to Miriam. "Mr. Schwarz seemed to think I could ignore the matter if I liked. At least, I assume that's what he meant by telling me Mr. Bronstein was not a member of the temple."

"Are you planning to?"

"Miriam!"

"Well, what are you going to do?"

"I'm not sure. I'll see him in any case. I suppose that will involve getting clearance from the authorities and probably from his lawyer as well. Perhaps it's even more important that I see Mrs. Bronstein."

"How about talking to Chief Lanigan?"

The rabbi shook his head. "What can I say to him? I know nothing about the case they have; I hardly know the Bronsteins. No, I'll call Mrs. Bronstein right now."

A woman answered and said that Mrs. Bronstein could not come to the telephone.

"This is Rabbi Small speaking. Would you ask her if it would be convenient for her to see me sometime today?"

"Will you hold the line a minute, please?" A moment later she returned to say that Mrs. Bronstein appreciated his calling, and would he make it sometime early in the afternoon?

"Tell her I'll be there at three o'clock."

He had no sooner hung up than the doorbell rang. It was Hugh Lanigan.

"I was just on my way back from the temple," he explained. "We've got something definite to check now. You heard about Bronstein?"

"I did, and the idea that he could have done this is utterly fantastic."

"You know him well, rabbi?"

"No, I don't."

"Well, before you go jumping to conclusions, let me tell you something: Mr. Bronstein was with the girl the night she was killed. That's not one of those fantastic mistakes the police make every now and then. He admits he was with her. He had dinner with her and he was with her all evening. He admits that, rabbi."

"Freely?"

Lanigan smiled. "You're thinking of a third degree, something in the nature of a rubber hose? I assure you we don't do that sort of thing here."

"No, I was thinking of questioning that might go on for hours on end, and little tongue slips being magnified until they are interpreted as admissions of guilt."

"You've got it all wrong, rabbi. As soon as he came to the station he made a statement. He could have refused to talk until he'd conferred with his lawyer, but he didn't. He said he had gone to the Surfside Restaurant and that he'd picked up the girl there. He claims he'd never seen her before. After dinner, they went to a movie in Boston and then had a bite. Afterwards, he drove her home and left her. That all seems pretty clear and straightforward, doesn't it? But the girl's body was found on Friday morning. Today is Monday. Four days later. If he was not involved, why didn't he come forward and give the police the information he had?"

"Because he's a married man. He was guilty of an indiscretion which suddenly ballooned up to monster proportions. It was very wrong of him not to go to the police, it was cowardly, it was unwise, but it still doesn't make him guilty of murder."

"That's just point number one, rabbi, but you'll admit it's enough to justify our picking him up for questioning. Here's point number two. The girl was pregnant. Mrs. Serafino, whom the girl worked for, was truly surprised to hear that; first, because she was a quiet girl who didn't run around, and secondly, because she never went out with men. In all the time she was with them, not once to Mrs. Serafino's knowledge did a man call for her, not once did she intimate or hint that she had been out with a man. On her evenings off, Thursdays, she would usually go to a movie, either alone or with a girlfriend who worked a few houses down. We questioned the girl, Celia, and she said that several times she had offered to fix Elspeth up with a man but each time she was refused. When Elspeth first came to town, Celia persuaded her to go to the Policemen and Firemen's Ball. All the housemaids go. That was the only time they went to a dance. Celia thought Elspeth might have a boyfriend back home in Canada—she got letters from time to time—that was the only way she could explain it. Celia was her only friend here and she certainly didn't get pregnant from Celia. So we did a little hunting and we found that your friend Mr. Bronstein had registered at least half a dozen times at various motels all along Route 14 and Route 69. He usually signed in under the name of Brown, and he was always with someone he registered as his wife. And as near as we can ascertain, it was always on a Thursday. We got positive identification of him by means of his picture and in one place by means of a penciled notation of his car license number. And a couple of the motel-keepers were pretty certain that his 'wife' was a blonde and that she resembled the picture we showed them of the murdered girl. That's point number two, rabbi."

"Did you tell him this about the motels?"

"Of course, or I wouldn't have told it to you."

"And what did he say?"

"He admits he was at those motels, but insists he wasn't there with this girl, that it was somebody else whose name he refuses to divulge."

"Well, if it's true—and it could be—that's rather admirable of him."

"Yes, if it's true. But we've got more. There is point three, which is not of too much significance but might be indicative. The girl went to see an obstetrician Thursday afternoon. She probably wore that wedding ring we found in her purse—for fairly obvious reasons. It was her first visit, so although she may have suspected her condition, she wasn't sure until Thursday. She gave her name as Mrs. Elizabeth Brown. And remember that Bronstein always registered as Mr. and Mrs. Brown."

"It's about as common as Smith," the rabbi observed.

"True."

"And nothing that you've said ties in with the fact the

girl had only a slip under her coat and raincoat. Quite the contrary. He must have taken her home as he said, because that is where she left her dress. I suppose there's no doubt that the coat and raincoat are hers, or that the dress she wore was found in her room.''

"That's right, and that brings us to point four. You've got to know the layout in the Serafino establishment in order to understand it. You don't know the Serafinos. I think I asked you once. Mr. Serafino operates a sort of nightclub. It's a small place where people sit around postage-stamp tables and drink watered-down liquor while Mr. Serafino sometimes plays the piano and his wife sings songs, risqué songs, bawdy songs, downright obscene songs. Not very nice people, you might say, but at home they're like any other young couple. They have two young children, and the family never misses a Sunday at church. The club doesn't close until two in the morning, so they need someone to take care of the children every night in the week, except Thursday, when Mrs. Serafino stays home and only her husband goes to the club. That's because Thursday is a slow night. It's maid's day off, so people, the kind that are apt to go to the Club Serafino, stay home. Anyway, the Serafinos need a live-in babysitter, which is not easy to come by for people in moderate circumstances. And in spite of what you might think of nightclub owners the Serafinos are people in moderate circumstances, and their house is arranged to meet their particular needs. It's two-story, and the Serafinos, Mr. and Mrs. and the two children, all sleep on the second floor. Off the kitchen on the first floor there's what amounts to a suite for the maid. She has a bedroom, small lavatory, a stall shower, and, most important, a private entrance. Do you get the picture?''

The rabbi nodded.

"Here we have an apartment that's almost completely separated from the rest of the house. Now what was to prevent our friend Mr. Bronstein from coming into the house with the girl—''

"And she took off her dress while he was in the room?''

"Why not? If our theory is right, she'd taken off more than her dress on previous occasions.''

"And then why did she go out again?"

Lanigan shrugged his shoulders. "I'll admit that here we're in the realm of pure conjecture. It's even possible that he strangled her right there in the room and then carried her out. A neighbor across the street who was beginning to get ready for bed looked out the window and saw Bronstein's blue Lincoln drive up to the Serafino house. That was shortly after twelve. Half an hour later he saw the Lincoln was still there. That's our fourth point."

"Did he see them get out of the car or get back in it?"

Lanigan shook his head.

"I know very little about these things," said the rabbi, "but as a Talmudist I am not entirely without legal training. Your theory has a thousand loopholes."

"Such as?"

"Such as the business of the coat and raincoat. If he had murdered her in her room, why did he then dress her up in a topcoat and then a raincoat? And why did he take her to the temple? And how did her handbag get into my car?"

"I've thought of all those objections, rabbi, and some others that you haven't mentioned, but I have more than enough to justify picking him up and holding him until we can check out a good many things. It's always that way. Do you think a case is ever presented to you with all the facts neatly explained? No, sir. You get a lead and you go to work on it. There are objections and you're aware of them, but as you keep digging you get answers to them, quite simple answers usually."

"And if you don't get the answers, after a while you release the man and his life is ruined," said the rabbi bitterly.

"True, rabbi. It's one of the penalties of living in organized society."

19

NATHAN GREENSPAN WAS A SCHOLARLY MAN, SLOW OF thought and speech. He sat behind his desk, and after poking his pipe with a spoonlike device, he blew through it once or twice to make sure it was drawing properly and then set about filling it very deliberately and methodically, while Becker, the inevitable cigar in his fist, strode up and down the room and told what had happened, what he suspected, and what he expected Greenspan to do. This last was something on the order of storming the police department and demanding that they release Bronstein immediately or face a suit for false arrest.

The lawyer put a match to his pipe, puffed at it until the entire surface was lit, and then firmly tamped down the burning tobacco that had risen in the bowl. He leaned back in his chair and spoke between puffs. "I can get a writ—of habeas corpus—if it seems that—he is being held unjustifiably—"

"Of course it's unjustifiable. He had nothing to do with it."

"How do you know?"

"Because he says so, and because I know him. You

know the kind of man Bronstein is. Does he look like a murderer to you?''

"According to what you've told me the police didn't arrest him for murder. They just took him in for questioning. He had information that they had a right to know—he said he had been out with her the night she was killed. Even if he hadn't, even if he only knew her or had ever gone out with her, the police would want to question him.''

"But they sent a couple of cops down to arrest him.''

"That's because he didn't come in on his own accord—as he should have, by the way.''

"All right, so he should have, but you know what that would have meant. I suppose he thought he could stay out of it entirely. So he was wrong, but that's no reason why he should be arrested and disgraced this way—cops coming to his house and hauling him off right in front of his wife.''

"It's common practice, Al. Anyway, it's done.''

"Well, what do you propose to do?''

"I'll go to see him, of course. They'll probably keep him overnight, but if they want to keep him any longer they're supposed to bring him before a judge and show probable cause. My guess is that they've got enough to hold him if they should want to. So my best bet, I imagine, would be to see the district attorney and see if I can find out just exactly what they have got on him.''

"Why can't you force them to release him if they can't prove he did it?''

Greenspan emitted a faint sigh. He put his pipe down on an ashtray and took off his glasses. "Look here, Al, a girl has been murdered. Right now, everybody is anxious to find the person who killed her. That means that every agency of the law is in sympathy with the police and that all laws and regulations will be stretched in their favor. Now if I start pulling legal tricks to get him off, everybody—and that includes the newspapers—is going to resent it. Mel wouldn't have a good press, and that won't do him any good no matter what happens. On the other hand, if we seem to be cooperative, the district attorney will give us whatever breaks he can.''

"And what do I do?''

"You don't do a darn thing, Al. You just practice being patient."

Patience, however, was one thing Al Becker did not have. He reasoned that if the conduct of the investigation depended on the attitude of the district attorney he could get quicker action by pressure from his friend Abe Casson, who had put the district attorney in office.

"What do you expect me to do, Al?" asked Casson. "I can tell you they've got a pretty good case against Mel right now. In fact, they could go to the grand jury with what they've got, but they're making it airtight."

"But he didn't do it, Abe."

"How do you know?"

"Because he told me. And because I know him."

Casson remained silent.

"Jesus, man, you know Mel Bronstein. Is he the kind of guy would do a thing like that? He's gentle as a girl. It doesn't make sense."

"These cases never make sense until they're over. Then they make lots of sense."

"Sure," said Becker bitterly. "If there's any little bit of evidence missing, they supply it. If there's a loophole, they plug it. Dammit, Abe, you know how these things work. They've got a lead, so they start chasing it down. They put every man on it. They know what they're trying to prove so they go ahead and prove it, until they get the poor bastard sewed up tight. And the real murderer goes free."

"What can I do, Al?"

"You're buddy-buddy with the D.A., to hear you tell it. You ought to be able to get him to keep his eyes open, to keep hunting for other possibilities."

Abe Casson shook his head. "The immediate investigation is in the hands of Chief Lanigan. You want to help your friend? Go see the rabbi."

"What in hell for? So that he can recite a prayer for him?"

"You know, Al, you've got an awfully big yap. Sometimes I think it's the only part of your head that works. Now listen to me. For some reason Hugh Lanigan has a great deal of respect for our rabbi. They're friendly. The other day, the rabbi and his wife spent the whole afternoon on Lanigan's porch. They were sitting there, the Lanigans and the Smalls, sipping drinks and talking."

"The rabbi never sat on my porch drinking and talking."

"Maybe you never invited him."

"All right, so let's say the chief likes him. What can the rabbi do for me?"

"He might do for you what you wanted me to do for you with the D.A."

"You think he would, knowing I'm the guy that's been working to get him out of here?"

"You believe he'd hold that against you in a matter of this sort? You don't know the rabbi. But if you want my advice—and really want to help your friend—that's what I suggest you do."

Miriam could scarcely pretend she was glad to see him. The rabbi greeted him formally. But Al Becker, if he was aware of the coolness of his reception, did not let it deter him. He fixed the rabbi with his most challenging glare and said, "Rabbi, Mel Bronstein could not possibly have done this terrible thing and you've got to do something about it."

"Anybody could possibly have done it," said the rabbi mildly.

"Yeah, I know," said Becker impatiently. "What I mean is that he's the last man in the world who would have done it. He's a sweet guy, rabbi. He's in love with his wife. They don't have any children. There are just the two of them and he's absolutely devoted to her."

"Do you know the nature of the evidence against him?" asked the rabbi.

"You mean he'd been playing around. So what? Do you know his wife has been in a wheelchair with multiple sclerosis for the last ten years of her life? For ten years they haven't had any—uh—relations."

"No, I didn't know that."

"A healthy man needs a woman. You being a rabbi wouldn't understand—"

"Rabbis aren't castrated."

"All right, I'm sorry. Then you know what I'm talking

138

about. The girls he went out with didn't mean that to Mel.'' He snapped his fingers. ''They were somebody he went to bed with, like he might go to a gym for a workout.''

''Well, I'm not sure they're precisely analogous, but that's beside the point. What do you want me to do?''

''I don't know. You were in your study all evening. Maybe you could say you happened to look out the window and saw a man drive out of the parking lot, and you can swear that it wasn't a blue Lincoln—''

''Are you asking me to perjure myself?''

''Jesus, pardon me, rabbi. I'm so upset I don't know what I'm saying. I'm going nuts with this business. This morning I lose a sale to a customer who's been buying Continentals from me every other year, regular like a calendar, for the last ten years. We come to terms Saturday and he's supposed to come in at noon to sign the contract. When he doesn't show, I call him and he tells me he's thinking of holding the old car for a little while longer and maybe he might go into a smaller car. You think business was bad for him this year? He had his biggest year. You know why he suddenly got cold on the deal? Fifteen years Mel and I have worked to build up this business, and now, overnight, it's going to pot.''

''Is it your business you are concerned about, or your friend?'' asked the rabbi coldly.

''It's everything. It's all mixed up in my mind. Mel wasn't only a partner or a friend—he was like a kid brother to me. And when you've spent fifteen years building up something, it isn't just another way of making a living. It's part of me. It's my life. It's to me what your profession is to you. And now my whole world has suddenly gone sour.''

''I can understand your position, Mr. Becker,'' said the rabbi, not unkindly, ''and I wish I could help. But you haven't come here to ask me to give your friend spiritual consolation. What you ask is utterly impossible. I'm afraid this business has warped your judgment, or you would realize that even if I were willing to do what you suggest, it would not be believed.''

''I know, I know. It's just that I'm desperate, rabbi.

But something you should be able to do. You're his rabbi, aren't you?''

"I have been led to believe I have been criticized for devoting my time to noncongregational matters," he observed quietly. "I understand that Mr. Bronstein is not a member of the congregation.''

Becker was angry now. "All right, so what? Does that mean you can't help him? He's a Jew, isn't he? He's a member of the Jewish community here in Barnard's Crossing and you're the only rabbi here. You can at least go to see him, can't you? You can at least see his wife. They're not members, you say. All right, so I am. Help me.''

"As a matter of fact," said the rabbi, "I already have an appointment to see Mrs. Bronstein and I was making arrangements to see Mr. Bronstein when you rang the bell.''

Becker was not stupid. He even managed a grin. "All right, rabbi, maybe I had that coming to me. What do you have in mind?''

"Chief Lanigan was here earlier and outlined the case against Mr. Bronstein. At the time, I thought the evidence admitted of another interpretation. But I don't really know the Bronsteins. So I thought I first ought to try to know them.''

"You'll never meet two nicer people, rabbi.''

"You realize how organizations work, Mr. Becker, and the police, I should imagine, are no different. They look everywhere until they find a suspect, but then they're likely to concentrate on him from then on. I thought I might be able to persuade Chief Lanigan not to stop looking elsewhere.''

"That's just what I had in mind, rabbi," said Becker ecstatically. "It's just what I said to Abe Casson. Ask him. I feel better already.''

20

THE JAIL CONSISTED OF FOUR SMALL STEEL-BARRED CELLS on the first floor of the Barnard's Crossing police station. Each cell had a narrow iron cot, a toilet, and a washbasin; a bulb in a porcelain socket dangled from the ceiling, suspended by a length of BX cable. A dim lamp burned day and night in the corridor, at one end of which was a barred window and at the other the wardroom. Beyond that was Lanigan's office.

From the wardroom, Hugh Lanigan showed the rabbi the cells and then led the way back to his office. "It isn't much of a jail," he said, "but fortunately it's all we need. I suppose it's one of the oldest jails in the country. This building goes back to Colonial times, and was originally used as the town hall. It's been fixed up of course, and renovated from time to time, but the foundation and most of the supporting beams are the original ones. And the cells have been modernized with electricity and flush toilets and running water, but they're still the original cells and they date back to before the Civil War."

"Where do the prisoners eat?" asked the rabbi.

Lanigan laughed. "We don't usually have them in the plural, except perhaps on Saturday night when we sometimes pick up a few drunk and disorderlies and let them sleep it off overnight. When we do have somebody in during mealtimes, one of the restaurants nearby, Barney Blake's usually, puts up a box lunch. In the old days, the police chief used to make a pretty good thing out of prisoners. The town allowed him a certain amount for each one kept overnight, plus a certain amount for each meal served. When I first joined the force, the chief was constantly after us patrolmen to bring in drunks. Anyone who stumbled on the street was apt to find himself locked up for the night. But some time ago long before I took over, the town upped the chief's salary and provided a regular allowance for feeding the prisoners, and I guess chiefs haven't been so anxious to make arrests since.''

"And your prisoners are confined to those little cells until they come up for trial?"

"Oh no. If we decide to charge your friend, we'll bring him up before a judge sometime tomorrow, and if he tells us to hold him the prisoner will be transferred to the jail in Salem or Lynn.''

"And are you planning to charge him?"

"That's pretty much up to the district attorney. We'll show him what we've got and maybe he'll ask some questions and then he'll make up his mind. He could decide not to charge him with the murder but to hold him as a material witness.''

"When will I be able to see him?"

"Right now, if you like. You can visit with him in his cell or see him right here in my office.''

"I think I'd rather see him alone, if you don't mind.''

"Oh, that's all right, rabbi. I'll have him brought in here and leave you two together.'' He laughed. "You're not carrying any weapons concealed about your person, are you? No files or hacksaws?''

The rabbi smiled and patted his jacket pockets. Lanigan went to the door that opened into the wardroom and shouted to one of the policemen to bring the prisoner into his office. Then he closed the door and left the rabbi alone. A moment later, Bronstein came in.

He seemed much younger than his wife, but the rabbi put that down to the difference in health rather than age. He was embarrassed.

"I sure appreciate your coming to see me, rabbi, but I'd give anything to have this meeting someplace else."

"Of course."

"You know, I found myself thinking that I was glad my parents were both dead—yes, and that I had no children. Because I wouldn't be able to face them, even when the police finally find the guilty person and let me go."

"I understand, but you must realize that misfortune can happen to anyone. Only the dead are safe from it."

"But this is so ugly . . ."

"All misfortune is ugly. You mustn't keep thinking about it. Tell me about the girl."

Bronstein did not answer immediately. He got up from his chair and paced the floor as if to gather his thoughts or to control his emotions. Then he stopped suddenly and faced the rabbi. He spoke in a rush:

"I never saw her before in my life. I'll swear that on my mother's grave. I've played around. I admit it. I suppose some people might say that if I loved my wife, I'd be completely faithful to her, even under the circumstances. Maybe I would have been if we'd had children, or maybe I could have if I were stronger. But what I have done, I'm willing to admit. I've had affairs with women, but there's never been anything serious or intense about them. And I've played fair with them. I never tried to hide the fact that I was married. I never handed a woman this line about my wife not understanding me. I never suggested that there was a possibility that I might divorce my wife. It was always straight forward and aboveboard. I had certain needs—my body had certain needs. Well, there are plenty of women who are in the same position and who use the same remedy. This woman that I shacked up with in motels a couple of times—it wasn't this kid. It's a married woman whose husband deserted her and she's filing for divorce."

"If you gave the police her name—"

Bronstein shook his head violently. "If I did that, it would interfere with her divorce. They might even take her children away. Don't worry, if it ever gets to the point where I'm actually put on trial, and it hinges on this, she'll come forward."

143

"You saw her every Thursday?"

"No, not last Thursday, and not for a couple of Thursdays before that. To tell the truth, she was getting edgy about our meeting. She got the idea that her husband might be having detectives trailing her."

"So that's how you came to pick up this girl—as a substitute?"

"I'll level with you, rabbi. When I picked her up, I wasn't planning any platonic friendship. I picked her up in a restaurant, the Surfside. If the police were really interested in getting the truth, rather than on pinning it on me, they'd inquire around among people who were there, the waitresses and the customers, and some of them would be sure to remember how I was sitting at one table and she at another, and how I went over to her and introduced myself. Anybody could see that it was a pick-up. But what I was going to say, was that after we had eaten together and talked for a while, I saw that the poor kid was frightened—frightened stiff, and trying awfully hard to be gay and not show it. Wouldn't that show she was expecting trouble?"

"Possibly. In any case, it's something worth looking into."

"I felt sorry for her. I just forgot about making a pass at her. I stopped being interested in her in that way. All I had in mind was a pleasant evening. We drove to Boston and went to a movie." He hesitated and then came to a quick decision. Leaning forward, he lowered his voice as though he were afraid of being overheard. "I'll tell you something I haven't told the police, rabbi. The silver chain that she wore, the one she was strangled with—God forgive me—I bought it for her just before we went into the show."

"You say you haven't told this to the police?"

"That's right. I'm not handing them anything they can use on me that I don't have to. The way they questioned me, they'd latch onto that as proof I was planning all evening to kill her. I'm telling you so you can see I'm leveling with you."

"All right. Then where did you go?"

"After the movie we dropped into a restaurant for

pancakes and coffee and then I drove her home. I drove right up to her house, parking right in front, all open and aboveboard."

"Did you go inside?"

"Of course not. We sat outside in the car for quite a while just talking. I didn't even put my arm around her. We just sat there and talked. Then she thanked me and got out of the car and went into the house."

"Did you make arrangements to meet her again?"

Bronstein shook his head. "I had a pleasant evening and I think she did too. She seemed a lot more relaxed by the time I took her home than she had at dinner. But there was no reason for me to repeat it."

"Then you went right home from there?"

"That's right."

"And your wife was asleep at the time?"

"I guess so. I sometimes think she only pretends to be asleep when I come home late. But anyway, she was in bed and the light was off."

The rabbi smiled. "That's the way she described it to me."

Bronstein looked up quickly. "You mean you've seen her? How is she? How is she taking all this?"

"Yes, I've seen her." In his mind's eye he could still visualize a thin, pale woman in a wheelchair, her hair just beginning to gray, brushed back from a high, unlined forehead; a nice-looking woman with finely carved features and gray eyes that were quick and bright.

"Her attitude was quite cheerful," said the rabbi.

"Cheerful?"

"I suppose she was making an effort, but I got the feeling that she was absolutely certain of your innocence. She said that if you had done this thing, she would have known it at a single glance."

"I don't suppose evidence like that would be of any use in court, rabbi, but it's true that we're very close to each other. In most marriages women get involved with their children, more or less to the exclusion of their husbands. But my wife got sick about ten years ago, and so we were together more than most couples. We can practically read each other. Do you understand, rabbi?"

145

The rabbi nodded.

"Of course, if she were only pretending to be asleep—"

"She said she always waited up for you, except on Thursdays. I thought perhaps it was because she was tired out from the excitement of entertaining her bridge club, but she assured me it wasn't that. It was because she knew you had been out with some woman and she didn't want to embarrass you."

"Oh my God." He covered his face with his hands.

The rabbi looked at him with pity and decided it was no time for preaching. "She was not hurt, she said. She understood."

"She said that? She said she understood?"

"Yes." The rabbi, uncomfortable at the turn of the conversation, tried to change it: "Tell me, Mr. Bronstein, does your wife ever leave the house?"

His face softened. "Oh yes, when the weather is nice and she feels up to it I take her for a ride. I like to drive, and I like to have her beside me. It's a little like old times then. You see, she's sitting there beside me just as she would be if she were well. There's no wheelchair to remind me that she's sick, although I have one, a collapsible one, in the trunk and sometimes on a warm night we drive over to the boulevard and I put her in it and walk her along the water."

"How does she get into the car?"

"I just pick her up and slide her onto the front seat."

The rabbi rose. "There are one or two points I think might be worth calling to the attention of the police. Maybe they can check into them if they haven't already done so."

Bronstein also rose. Hesitantly he offered his hand "Believe me, rabbi, I appreciate your coming here."

"Do they treat you all right?"

"Oh yes." He nodded in the direction of the cells. "After I finished answering their questions they left the door of the cell unlocked so I could walk up and down the corridor if I wanted to. Some of the policemen have been in to chat and they gave me some magazines to read. I wonder—"

"Yes?"

"I wonder if you could get word to my wife that I'm all right. I wouldn't want her to worry."

The rabbi smiled. "I'll be in touch with her, Mr. Bronstein."

21

AS HE LEFT BRONSTEIN, THE RABBI REFLECTED SADLY THAT his first attempts to help had succeeded only in uncovering two points, both minor and both detrimental to the unfortunate man. In his interview with Mrs. Bronstein he had learned that on this one night of the week she had not been up to greet her husband. Of course even if she could say he had not seemed upset, it would not help much; as his wife she would not be given full credence, and in any case it was only negative evidence. Amd what stuck in his mind from his interview with the husband was the picture of him scooping his wife up in his arms and depositing her on the car seat. He had always thought it might be difficult and awkward for the murderer to carry the body from one car to the other, but now Mel Bronstein had demonstrated it would be no trick at all, that he was a practiced hand at it.

Bronstein's car was a big Lincoln, whereas his was a compact, which could make a difference. When he got home, he drove into the garage, got out, and studied the car, a frown on his thin, scholarly face. Then he called into the house for Miriam to come out for a minute.

She did so, standing beside him and following the direction of his stare. "Did someone scratch it?"

Instead of answering, he put his arm around her waist absently. She smiled affectionately at him, but he did not appear to notice. He reached out and swung open the car door.

"What is it, David?"

He pulled at his lower lip as he surveyed the interior of the car. Then, without a word, he bent down and picked her up in his arms.

"David!"

He staggered with his burden over to the open car door.

She began to giggle.

He tried to ease her onto the seat. "Let your head hang back," he ordered.

Instead, still giggling, she wrapped her arms around his neck and put her face against his.

"Please, Miriam."

She pecked at his ear.

"I'm trying to—"

She swung her legs provocatively. "What would Mr. Wasserman say if he saw us now?"

"Having fun?"

They turned to see Chief Lanigan in the doorway, a broad smile on his face.

The rabbi hastily set his wife down. He felt foolish. "I was just experimenting," he explained. "It's not easy to maneuver a body onto a car seat."

Lanigan nodded. "No, but although the girl probably weighed more than Mrs. Small, Bronstein's a good bit bigger than you."

"I suppose that makes a difference," the rabbi said, as he led the way into the house and to his study.

When they were seated, Lanigan asked how he had made out with Bronstein.

"I got to know him this afternoon," said the rabbi. "He's not the sort of person who would be likely to do a thing like this—"

"Rabbi, rabbi," the chief interrupted impatiently, "when you've seen as many criminals as I have you'll know that appearances are meaningless. Do you suppose a thief has a furtive look? Or that a confidence man is shifty-eyed? Why, his stock in trade is an open, frank appearance and an ability to look you straight in the eye. You people are called the People of the Book, and I suppose a rabbi is a particularly bookish sort of person. I have a great deal of respect for books and for bookish people, rabbi, but in matters such as this it's experience that counts."

"But if appearances and manner are deceptive, then all appearances are neutralized," said the rabbi mildly, "and it's hard to see how a jury system could possibly function. What do you base your convictions on?"

"Evidence, rabbi. On mathematically certain evidence, if it's available, or on the weight of probabilities if it isn't."

The rabbi nodded slowly. Then he said with seeming irrelevance, "Do you know about our Talmud?"

"That's your book of laws, isn't it? Does it have anything to do with this?"

"Well, it's not really our book of laws. The Books of Moses are that. It's the commentaries on the Law. I don't suppose it has any direct connection with the case at hand, but you can't be too sure of that either since all kinds of things can be found in the Talmud. I wasn't thinking at the moment of its contents, however, but rather of the method of its study. When I began to study in the religious school as a youngster, all subjects—Hebrew, grammar, literature, the Scriptures—all were taught in the ordinary way, just as subjects are taught in the public school. That is to say, we sat at desks while the teacher sat at a larger desk on a platform. He wrote on the board, he asked questions, he gave out home lessons and heard us recite. But when I began Talmud, instruction was different. Imagine a large table with a group of students around it. At the head of the table was the teacher, a man with a long, patriarchal beard in this case. We read a passage, a short statement of the Law. Then followed the objections, the explanations, the arguments of the rabbis of old on the proper interpretation of the passage. Before we quite knew what we were doing, we were adding our own arguments, our own objections, our own hair-splitting distinctions and twists of logic, the so-called pilpul. Sometimes the teacher took it on himself to defend a given position and then we peppered him with questions and objections. I imagine a bear-baiting must have been like that—a shaggy bear surrounded by a pack of yelping dogs, and the moment he manages to toss off one another is ready to charge. As you begin to argue, new ideas keep presenting themselves. I remember an early passage I studied, which considered how damages should be assessed in the case of a fire resulting from a spark that flew out from under the blacksmith's hammer. We spent two whole weeks on that one passage, and when we finally reluctantly left it, it was with the feeling that we had barely begun. The study of the Talmud has exercised a tremendous influence over us. Our great scholars spent their lives studying the Talmud, not because the exact interpretation of the Law happened to be germane to their problems at the time—in many cases the particular laws had become dead letters—but because as a mental exercise it had a tremendous fascination for them. It encouraged them to dredge up from their minds all kinds of ideas—"

"And you propose to use this method on our present problem?"

"Why not? Let's examine the weight of probabilities in your theory and see if it stands up."

"All right, go ahead."

The rabbi got up from his chair and began to stride about the room. "We will start not with the body, but with the handbag."

"Why?"

"Why not?"

Lanigan shrugged his shoulders. "Okay, you're the teacher."

"Actually, the handbag is a more fertile field of investigation if only because it touches on three people. The body lying behind the wall concerns only two people: the girl and her murderer. The handbag involves those two and me, because it was in my car that the handbag was found."

"Good enough."

"Now, what are the possibilities by which the handbag could have been left where it was found? It could have been left by the girl or by the man who killed her,

151

or by a third party, unknown, unsuspected, and until now unconsidered.''

"You got something new up your sleeve, rabbi?" asked Lanigan suspiciously.

"No, I'm merely considering all the possibilities.''

There was a knock on the study door and Miriam came in with a tray.

"I thought you'd like some coffee," she said.

"Thank you," said Lanigan. "Aren't you going to join us?" he said when he noticed there were only two cups on the tray.

"May I?"

"Certainly. There's nothing very confidential about this. The rabbi is just giving me my first lesson in the Talmud.''

When she returned with a coffee cup, he said, "All right, rabbi, we've listed all the people who could have left the handbag. Where does that take us?"

"Of course the first question that comes to mind is why she had the bag with her at all. I suppose it's automatic with some women.''

"A lot of women attach their house key to the inside of the bag by a chain," suggested Mrs. Small.

Lanigan nodded to her. "Good guess. That's how she had her key, attached by a short chain to the ring that's the zipper-pull for an inside pocket.''

"So she took the bag rather than go to the trouble of detaching the key," the rabbi went on. "Now let's consider one by one the people who could possibly have left it in my car. First, to clear him out of the way, the third party, the unsuspected stranger. He would be someone who happened to be walking along and saw the bag, presumably because it was lying on the ground somewhere near the car. He would certainly open it, if only to find out if there was any identification so he could return it to its proper owner. But, more likely, he would open it out of common curiosity. If he were dishonest, he would have taken whatever of value it contained. But he did not do this.''

"How do you know that, rabbi?" asked Lanigan, suddenly alert.

"Because you said you found a heavy gold wedding

ring. If the man were dishonest, he would have taken it. That he did not, suggests to me that any other thing of value—money, for instance—was left undisturbed."

"There was some money in the purse," Lanigan admitted. "About what you'd expect, a couple of bills and some loose change."

"Very good. So we can assume it is not the case of someone finding the purse, taking out whatever was of value, and then tossing away the bag itself, now valueless, so that it would not be found on him."

"All right, where does that get you?"

"It merely clears the ground. Now suppose he were honest and wanted only to return it to its rightful owner, and he put it in my car because he had found it nearby and assumed it belonged there, or because he thought the driver, finding it in his car, would take the trouble to return it to the rightful party. If that were his sole connection with the bag, why did he put it on the floor in back instead of on the front seat, where the driver would be sure to find it? I could have driven around for days without seeing it."

"All right, so a hitherto unsuspected stranger did not leave the bag in the car, neither an honest one nor a dishonest one. I never said one did."

"So we'll go on to the next. We'll take the girl."

"The girl is out. She was dead at the time."

"How can you be so sure? It would seem that the most likely explanation for the handbag is that the girl herself left it in the car."

"Look here, it was a warm night and you must have had the window of your study open. Right?"

"Yes. The window was up, but the venetian blinds were down."

"How far do you think you were from your car? I'll tell you. The car was twenty feet away from the building. Your study is on the second floor, say eleven feet above ground level. Add another four feet to give you the height of the windowsill. Now if you remember your high-school geometry, the line from the car to you is the hypotenuse of a right triangle. And if you work it out, you'll find that the sill was about twenty-five feet away from the car. Add ten feet to give you your position at your desk. That means you were thirty-five feet from the car. And if someone had got into that car, let alone quarreled and got murdered in it, you'd have heard it no matter how engrossed you were in your studies."

"But it could have happened after I left the temple," the rabbi objected.

Lanigan shook his head. "Not too easily. You said you left sometime after twelve. You figured out it was about twenty past. But Patrolman Norman was walking up Maple Street towards the temple, and about that time or very shortly thereafter he was within sight of the temple. The parking lot was under his observation from that time up to three minutes past one when he pulled the box on the corner. Then he headed down Vine Street, which is the street the Serafinos live on and was therefore the street the girl must have come down."

"All right, then after that?" suggested the rabbi.

Lanigan shook his head again. "Nothing doing. The medical examiner first reported that the girl was killed around one o'clock, with a twenty-minute leeway either side. But that was on the basis of body temperature, rigidity, and so forth. When we questioned Bronstein we discovered they'd eaten after the movie, and that enabled the M.E. to make a determination of the time on the basis of stomach content, which is a good deal more accurate. He gave us a supplementary report that fixes one o'clock at the outside."

"Then in that case we have to consider the possibility that in spite of my proximity to the car I was so engrossed that I heard nothing. Remember, the car windows were up, and if they were careful in opening and closing the car door and if they conversed in low tones I wouldn't have heard them. Also, the way she was killed, by strangulation, would have prevented her from crying out."

Lanigan pointed at the rabbi's head. "What do you call that thing you're wearing?"

The rabbi touched his black silk skullcap. "This? A *kipoh*."

"Then forgive me, rabbi," he said, grinning, "but you're talking through your *kipoh*. Why would they be careful about opening and closing the car doors and keeping their voices down to a whisper when they had no reason to assume anyone was within earshot? If they were there before it began to rain, they would have lowered the windows. It was warm, remember. And if it was during the rain, Norman surely would have seen them. What's more, there was no indication the girl had been in your car. Look here." He opened his dispatch case and took out some papers, which he spread on the rabbi's desk, and they all drew near to look. "These are the total contents of your car—a list of what was in every receptacle. Here's a diagram of the interior of the car showing where each item was found. Here's where the handbag was found, on the floor under the seat. Here in the plastic trash pocket were lipstick-stained tissues, but it was your wife's lipstick. On the floor in the rear, right behind the front seats, there was a bobby pin but it was your wife's. There were a number of cigarette butts in the front ashtray and one in the rear ashtray, and all were lipstick-stained with your wife's lipstick, and it was the brand she smokes because they're the same as the partially filled pack we found in the glove compartment."

"Just a minute," said Miriam, "that one in the rear ashtray can't be mine. I've never sat in the back seat since we got the car."

"What's that? Never sat in the back seat? That's impossible."

"Is it?" asked the rabbi mildly. "I have never sat in any seat but the driver's seat. Actually, the back seat has never been used, come to think of it. Since we got the car, less than a year ago, I have never had occasion to transport anyone. When I am in the car, I am in the driver's seat, and when Miriam comes along she sits beside me. What is so strange about that? How often do you sit in the back seat of your car?"

"But it must have got there somehow. The lipstick is your wife's, the brand of cigarette is hers. Look here, here's a list of what was in the girl's handbag. No cigarettes, you notice."

The rabbi studied the list. Then he pointed. "But there's a cigarette lighter, and that would indicate that she smoked. As far as the lipstick goes, you said it was the same brand and shade as Miriam's. After all, they're both blondes."

"Just a minute," said Lanigan. "The bobby pin was found in the back of the car, so you must have—"

Miriam shook her head. "Sitting in the front seat, it would be in the back that the pin would fall."

"Yes, I suppose so," said Lanigan, "but it still doesn't give us what you'd call a clear picture. She had no cigarettes—at least there were none in her purse, right?"

"Right, but she was not alone. There was someone with her—the murderer—and he probably had cigarettes."

"Are you saying that the girl was murdered in your car, rabbi?"

"Precisely. The lipstick-stained cigarette in the rear ashtray proves that a woman was in the rear seat of my car. The handbag on the floor in the rear shows that it was Elspeth Bleech."

"All right, let's say she was there. Let's even grant she was killed in your car. How does that help Bronstein?"

"I'd say it clears him."

"You mean because he had a car of his own?"

"Yes. Why would he drive into the parking lot with the girl, park alongside my car, and then change cars?"

"He might have killed her in his own car and then transferred the body to your car."

"You're forgetting the cigarette in the rear ashtray. She was alive in my car."

"Suppose he forced her into your car."

"For what reason?"

Lanigan shrugged. "Perhaps to avoid having any signs of struggle in his own car."

"You're not giving that cigarette its full weight as evidence. If she smoked that cigarette in the rear seat of my car, then she was at ease. No one had his hand at her throat—no one was threatening her. For that matter, if after taking off her dress she had to go back to Bronstein's car for some reason, why would she have put on the raincoat?"

"Because it was raining, of course."

The rabbi shook his head impatiently. "The car was right in front of the house. How far? Fifty feet? She had put on a topcoat to cover her slip, and that certainly was protection enough against the rain for such a short run.''

Lanigan rose and began to pace the floor. The rabbi watched him, unwilling to interrupt his train of thought. But when he continued silent, the rabbi said, "Bronstein should have come to the police as soon as he found out what happened, admitted. For that matter, he shouldn't have picked up the girl in the first place. But even if you can't condone it, it is understandable in the light of the situation at home. And again you can't condone his withholding information from the police, but you can understand it. Arresting him for questioning, with its attendant publicity, is more than enough punishment, don't you agree? Chief Lanigan, take my advice and let him go.''

"But that would leave me without a suspect.''

"That's not like you.''

"What do you mean?'' The chief's face reddened.

"I can't imagine you holding a man just so that you can report progress to the press. Besides, it will only hamper your investigation. You'll find yourself thinking about Bronstein, trying to evolve theories that put him in the picture, checking his past, interpreting whatever new evidence comes up, from the point of view of his possible involvement. And that's obviously the wrong direction for your investigation to take.''

"Well . . .''

"Don't you see, you've got nothing on him other than his failure to come forward.''

"But the D.A. is coming down in the morning to question him.''

"Then tell him he'll turn up voluntarily. I'll go bond for him. I'll guarantee his appearance when you want him.''

Lanigan picked up his dispatch case. "All right, I'll let him go." He went to the door, and with his hand on the knob he paused. "Of course, rabbi, you realize that you haven't exactly improved your own position.''

22

AL BECKER WAS NOT ONE TO FORGET A FAVOR. THE MORN-
ing after his partner was released, he went to see Abe
Casson to thank him personally for his good offices in
the matter.

"Yeah, I spoke to the district attorney but I didn't get
far. As I told you, this case is being handled pretty much
by the local police, at least so far."

"Is that customary?"

"Well, it is and it isn't. The lines of authority aren't
clearly drawn. The state detectives usually come in on
murders. The district attorney in whose county a major
crime is committed and whose office will have to prose-
cute, he's in on it. Then the local police, because they
know local conditions, they have a hand in it. It depends
a lot on the character of the local police chief and on the
character of the D.A. and what men are available and
what special issues are at stake. You take in a big city
like Boston, it would be the Boston police who'd be
running the show because they have the men and they're
equipped for it. Now down here, the investigation is
being run pretty much by Hugh Lanigan. Mel was picked
up on his orders and he was released on his orders. And
I'll tell you something else: Lanigan released him as a

result of some new angle or some new interpretation of the evidence that the rabbi showed him. That's not customary, if you like—I mean, a cop giving someone else the credit for some clever detective work—but then Hugh Lanigan is no ordinary cop."

Al Becker did not take Abe Casson's remarks at face value. He did not doubt that the rabbi had spoken to Lanigan about the matter—conceivably, in the course of the conversation, some chance remark of the rabbi's may have given the police chief a different slant—but he did not believe the rabbi had been able to work out a convincing defense of his friend. Still, he supposed he ought to see the rabbi and thank him.

Once again, their meeting was not without its awkwardness. Becker came straight to the point. "I understand that you had a lot to do with Mel Bronstein's being released, rabbi."

It would have been easier had the rabbi made the expected modest disclaimer, but instead he said, "Yes, I suppose I did."

"Well, you know how I feel about Mel. He's like a kid brother to me. So you can understand how grateful I am. I haven't exactly been one of your most active supporters—"

The rabbi smiled. "And now you are somewhat embarrassed. There's no need to be, Mr. Becker. I'm sure your objection was in no way personal. You feel that I'm not the right man for the position I hold. You have every right to go on feeling that way. I helped your friend as I would help you or anyone else who needed it, just as I'm sure you would in like circumstances."

Becker phoned Abe Casson to report on his conversation with the rabbi, ending with, "He's a hard man to like. I went there to thank him for helping Mel and to more or less apologize for having worked against him on the contract business, and he as much as told me he didn't need my friendship and didn't care if I continued to oppose him."

"That's not the impression I got from your story. You know, Al, maybe you're too smart to understand a man like the rabbi. You're used to reading between the lines and guessing what people really mean. Has it ever occurred to you that the rabbi might not talk between the lines, that he says pretty much exactly what he means?''

"Well, I know you and Jake Wasserman and Abe Reich are sold on him. The rabbi can do no wrong as far as you people are concerned, but—"

"He seems to have done all right for you too, Al."

"Oh, I'm not saying that he didn't do me and Mel a favor, and I'm grateful. But you know very well that Mel would have got off anyway, maybe in another day or two, because they didn't have a thing on him."

"Don't be so sure. You don't know how they play the game. In an ordinary case where a man is tried for some ordinary crime—sure, the chances are that if he's innocent he'll go free. But in a case of this kind there's another element. It's no longer just a case at law. Politics enters into it, and then they're not so concerned about whether a man is guilty or not. They start thinking in different terms: have we got enough to go before a jury with? If the man is innocent, let his lawyer take care of him and if he doesn't, it's just too bad. It becomes a sort of game, like football, with the D.A. on one side and the defendant's lawyer on the other, and the judge the referee. And the defendant? He's the football.''

"Yes, but—''

"And another thing, Al, if you really want to see this in its proper perspective, just ask yourself what happens now? Who's the chief suspect? I'll tell you—it's the rabbi. Now whatever your opinion of the rabbi, you can't call him stupid. So you can be sure he knows that in getting Bronstein off the hook he was putting himself squarely on. Think about that for a while, Al, and then ask yourself again if the rabbi is such a hard man to like.''

23

Sunday it rained. The rain had started early in the morning, and the corridor and classrooms of the Sunday school were pervaded with the smell of wet raincoats and rubbers. Mr. Wasserman and Abe Casson, standing just inside the outer door, stared moodily at the parking lot, watching raindrops bounce against the shiny asphalt.

"It's a quarter-past ten, Jacob," said Casson. "It doesn't look as though we're going to have a meeting today."

"A little bit of rain, and they're afraid to go out."

They were joined by Al Becker. "Abe Reich and Meyer Goldfarb are here, but I don't think you'll be getting many more."

"We'll wait another fifteen minutes," said Wasserman.

"If they're not here now, they won't be here," said Casson flatly.

"Maybe we should make a few telephone calls," Wasserman suggested.

"If they're afraid of a little rain," said Becker, "your calling them won't change their minds."

Casson snorted derisively. "You think that's what's keeping them away?"

"What else?"

161

"I think the boys are playing it cozy. Don't you understand, Al? They don't any of them want to get mixed up in this."

"Mixed up in what?" demanded Becker. "What the hell are you talking about?"

"I'm talking about a girl who was murdered. And about the rabbi's possible connection with her. We were supposed to vote today on the rabbi's new contract, remember? And I imagine some of the boys started to think about the possibilities. Suppose they vote for keeping the rabbi, and then it turns out he's guilty. What would their friends say, especially their Gentile friends? What would be the effect on their business? Now do you get it?"

"It never occurred to me," Becker began slowly.

"That's because it probably never occurred to you that the rabbi could have done it," said Casson. He looked at Becker curiously. "Tell me, Al, didn't you get any phone calls?"

Becker looked blank, but Wasserman's face began to color.

"Ah, I see you got some, Jacob," Casson went on.

"What kind of calls?" asked Becker.

"Tell him, Jacob."

Wasserman shrugged his shoulders. "Who pays attention? Cranks, fools, bigots, am I going to listen to them? I hang up on them."

"And you've been getting them. too?" Becker demanded of Casson.

"Yeah. I imagine they called Jacob because he's president. And they called me because I'm in politics and so I'm known."

"And what have you done about it?" demanded Becker.

Casson shrugged his shoulders. "Same as Jacob—nothing. What can you do about it? When the murderer is found, it'll stop."

"Well, something ought to be done about it. At least we ought to tell the police or the Selectmen or—"

"And what can they do? Now if I were to recognize a voice, that would be something else again."

"Yeah."

"It's new to you, eh? And it's probably new to Jacob. But it's not new to me. I've had this type of call in every political campaign. The world is full of nuts—bitter, disappointed, disturbed men and women. Individually, they're mostly harmless. Collectively, they're kind of unpleasant to think about. They write nasty obscene letters to the newspapers or to people whose names are mentioned in the news, and if it happens to be someone local, they telephone."

Wasserman looked at his watch. "Well, gentlemen, a meeting I'm afraid we won't have today."

"It wouldn't be the first time we didn't get a quorum," said Becker.

"And what do I tell the rabbi? That he should wait another week? And next week, we are sure we'll get a quorum?" He looked quizzically at Becker.

Becker colored. Then suddenly he was angry. "So if we don't get a quorum, it'll be next week, or the following week, or the week after that. You've got the votes. Does he need it in writing?"

"There's also the little matter of the opposition votes that you mustered," Casson reminded him.

"You don't have to worry about them now," said Becker stiffly. "I told my friends I was in favor of renewing the rabbi's contract."

Hugh Lanigan dropped by that evening to see the rabbi.

"I thought I'd congratulate you on your reprieve. According to my source of information, the opposition to you has collapsed."

The rabbi smiled noncommittally.

"You don't seem very happy about it," said Lanigan.

"It's a little like getting in through the back door."

"So that's it. You think you're getting this reappointment or election, or whatever it is, because of what you were able to do for Bronstein. Well, here, I am in a position to teach you, rabbi. You Jews are skeptical, critical, and logical."

"I always thought we were supposed to be highly emotional," said the rabbi.

"And so you are, but only about emotional things.

163

You Jews have no political sense whatsoever, and we Irish have a genius for it. When you argue or campaign for office, you fight on the issues. And when you lose, you console yourselves with the thought you fought on the issues and argued reasonably and logically. It must have been a Jew who said he'd rather be right than President. An Irishman knows better; he knows that you can do nothing unless you're elected. So the first principle of politics is to get elected. And the second great principle is that a candidate is not elected because he's the logical choice, but because of the way he has his hair cut, or the hat he wears, or his accent. That's the way we pick even the President of the United States, and for that matter, that's the way a man picks his wife. Now wherever you have a political situation, political principles apply. So don't you worry as to why or how you were chosen. You just be happy that you were chosen.''

"Mr. Lanigan is right, David," said Miriam. "We know that if your contract had not been renewed you could have got another position as good or better than this, but you like it here in Barnard's Crossing. Besides, Mr. Wasserman is sure the raise will be granted, and we can find some use for that."

"That's already spoken for, my dear," said the rabbi hurriedly.

She made a face. "More books?"

He shook his head. "Not this time. When this business is finally over, I'm going to apply the extra money toward a new car. The thought of that poor girl . . . Every time I get into the car I almost shudder. I find myself thinking up excuses for walking instead of riding."

"Understandable," said Lanigan, "but maybe you'll feel differently once we find the murderer."

"Oh? How does it look?"

"We're getting new material all the time. We're working around the clock. Right now, we've got some promising leads."

"Or to put it another way," said the rabbi, "you're at a dead end."

Lanigan's answer was a shrug and a wry grin.

"If you want my advice," said Miriam, "you'll put it out of your mind and have a cup of tea."

164

"That's sound advice," said Lanigan.

They sipped their tea and talked about the town, politics, the weather—the aimless, idle conversation of people who had nothing weighing on their minds. Lanigan finally rose with obvious reluctance.

"It's been very pleasant just sitting here and talking, rabbi, Mrs. Small, but I've got to get back now."

Just as he was leaving, the telephone rang, and although the rabbi was nearest his wife ran to answer. She said hello, and then listened for a moment, the receiver pressed firmly against her ear. "I'm sorry, you have the wrong number," she said firmly and hung up.

"We seem to be getting quite a few wrong numbers the last couple of days," observed the rabbi.

Lanigan, his hand on the doorknob, looked from the rabbi, his face innocent and bland, to his wife, her cheeks pink with embarrassment? with annoyance? with anger? In response to his questioning look he thought he detected an almost imperceptible shake of her head, so with a smile and a wave of his hand he let himself out.

Night after night pretty much the same group sat in the circular booth down front at the Ship's Cabin. Sometimes there were as many as six, most nights only three or four. They called themselves the Knights of the Round Table and were inclined to be noisy and boisterous. Although Alf Cantwell, the proprietor of the tavern, was strict and prided himself on running an orderly establishment, he was likely to be lenient with them because they were regular customers, and if they did occasionally get quarrelsome they kept it within the confines of their own circle. Even then, on the two or three occasions he had had to order his barman to stop serving them and had in fact told them to leave, they had taken it in good part and had come back the following evening without rancor and a little repentant: "Guess we were a little high last night, Alf. Sorry, won't happen again."

There were four of them at the table when Stanley came in at half-past nine Monday. Buzz Applebury, a tall, lean man with a long nose, hailed him as he entered. He was a painter-contractor who had his own shop, and Stanley had worked for him on occasion.

"Hi, Stan'l," he called, "come on over and have a drink."

"Well . . ." Stanley temporized. They were a cut above him socially. In addition to Applebury there was Harry Cleeves who had an appliance repair shop, Don Winters who operated a small grocery store, and Malcolm Larch who had a real estate and insurance office. These men were all merchants, whereas he was a laborer.

"Sure, come on and sit down, Stan'l," Larch urged and moved over on the circular bench to make room for him. "What'll you have to drink?"

They were drinking whiskey, but his customary drink was ale and he did not want them to think he was taking advantage of their hospitality.

"I'll have ale," he said.

"Attaboy, Stan'l, you keep sober because maybe we'll need you to take us home."

"Beauty," said Stanley in appreciation.

Harry Cleeves, a blond giant with a round baby face, had been staring moodily at his glass all this time and had paid no attention to Stanley. Now he turned around and addressed him with an air of great seriousness. "You still work up at the Jew church?"

"At the temple? Yeah, I still work there."

"You been there a long time now," Applebury observed.

"Couple—three years," said Stanley.

"You wear one of them dinky little hats they wear when they pray?"

"Sure, when they're having a service and I'm on duty."

Applebury turned to the others. "When they're having a service and he's on duty, he says."

"How do you know that don't make you a Jew?" asked Winters.

Stanley looked quickly from one to the other. Deciding they were joking, he laughed and said, "Jeez, Don, that don't make you no Jew."

"Of course not, Don," said Applebury, looking down his long nose reprovingly at his friend. "Everybody knows they got to cut off your whatsis to make you a Jew. They cut you off, Stan'l?"

Stanley was sure this was intended as a joke and laughed accordingly. "Beauty," he added to indicate his full appreciation of the jest.

"You want to watch out, Stan'l," Winters went on, "you might get so smart associating with them Jews you'll just naturally stop working."

"Oh, they ain't so smart," said Applebury. "I did a job of work for one of them up on the Point. They ask me for an estimate, so I give them a figure a third higher than the job is worth, calculating on coming down in the dicker. But this Jew fellow just says, Go ahead but do a good job. At that, what with his wife wanting the colors just so, and Would you make this wall just a shade darker than the other, Mr. Applebury? and Could you make the woodwork perfectly flat, Mr. Applebury?—why, maybe it was worth the difference at that. She was a real nice little woman," he added reminiscently. "She wore those tight black pants—toreador pants, I guess they call them—and her little arse wiggled so when she walked I couldn't keep my mind on my work."

"I heard that Hugh Lanigan was setting up to become one," said Harry Cleeves. The others laughed, but he seemed not to notice. Suddenly he turned to Stanley. "How about that, Stan'l? You hear anything about any preparations they were making down there to swear Hugh Lanigan in?"

"Naw."

"Now Harry, I heard something about that," said Malcolm Larch. "It ain't that Hugh's planning to join them. It's just this business about the girl. I figure Hugh is working with this rabbi of theirs to make sure no evidence gets out that would show that the rabbi did it."

"How could he do that?" asked Cleeves. "If the rabbi did it, how's Hugh going to cover up for him?"

"Well, the way I heard it, he tried to pin it onto this Bronstein fellow instead, on account Bronstein wasn't a member of their outfit. But then it turns out that he's connected with one of their high officers so they had to let him go. Those in the know figure they'll try to pin it on some outsider next. Hugh been bothering you any, Stan'l?" He turned to him innocently.

Stanley knew they were pulling his leg now, but instead of finding it amusing he felt uneasy. He forced a grin. "No, Hugh don't pay me no mind."

"What I don't understand," said Cleeves reflectively, "is what this rabbi would want to kill that little girl for."

"Somebody was saying, but it didn't seem too likely, that it's part of the religion," explained Winters.

"I don't figure there's much in that," said Larch, "at least not around these parts. Maybe in Europe, or in some big city like New York where they're powerful and could get away with it, but not around here."

"Then what would he want with a young girl like that?" demanded Winters.

"She was pregnant, wasn't she?" Cleeves turned suddenly to Stanley. "Isn't that what he wanted her for, Stan'l?"

"Aw, you guys are nuts," said Stanley.

They laughed, but Stanley did not feel the atmosphere lighten. He felt uncomfortable.

Larch said, "Hey Harry, didn't you have to make a telephone call?"

Cleeves glanced at his wristwatch. "It's a little late, isn't it?"

"The later the better, Harry." He winked at his friends, and said, "Ain't that right, Stan'l?"

"Guess so."

This caused renewed laughter. Stanley kept a fixed grin on his face. He wanted to leave but did not know how. They all watched, not talking now, as Cleeves dialed a number and then talked on the phone. A few minutes later he came out and made an O with his thumb and forefinger to indicate that the call had been successful.

Stanley got up so that Cleeves could regain his seat. Standing, he realized that this was the time to break away. "Got to go now," he said.

"Aw, c'mon, Stan'l, have another."

"The night's young, Stan'l."

"Shank of the evening—"

Applebury grabbed his arm, but Stanley shook him off and made for the door.

24

Carl Macomber, chairman of the Board of Selectmen of Barnard's Crossing, was by nature a worrier. A tall, spare man with gray hair, he had been in town politics for forty years, and on the Board of Selectmen for almost half that time. The two hundred and fifty dollars per year that he received, fifty dollars more than the other members, for being chairman was certainly inadequate compensation for the three or more hours a week he spent in attending Board meetings all through the year, the dozens of hours he spent on town business, and the hectic weeks of campaigning every other year if he wanted to be re-elected.

There was no doubt that his business—he operated a small haberdashery—had suffered from his devotion to politics. Every election he and his wife had extensive debates about whether he should run again, and convincing her, he often said, was the biggest hurdle of the campaign.

"But, Martha, I've simply got to remain on the Board now that the question of taking over the Dollop Estate by eminent domain is coming up. There just isn't anyone else who knows the ins and outs of that business except me. If Johnny Wright would run, I could stay out. But he's going to Florida for the winter. He was the only one besides me who was in on the negotiations with the heirs back in '52. And if I should drop out now, I'd hate to think how much it would cost the town.''

Before that it had been the new school, and before that the new sanitation and health department, and before that the wage survey of town employees, and before that something else. Sometimes he wondered about it himself. The unbending Yankee in him would not permit him to admit to himself anything so sentimental as love for the town. Instead, he told himself that he liked to be in the middle of things and know what was going on, and that it was his duty since he could do the job better than any of the other candidates.

Running the town wasn't just a matter of dealing with questions as they came up, he always said; by that time it was too late. Rather, it involved a crisis in the making and forestalling it. Such was the situation right now with respect to Rabbi Small and the Temple Murder, as the newspapers had labeled the case. It wasn't anything he cared to discuss at the regular meeting of the Board. Even the five members were too many when all he needed was a majority of three to railroad anything they decided through an official meeting with a minimum of discussion.

He had called Heber Nute and George Collins, the two older members of the Board, and next to himself the oldest in length of service. They were sitting now in his living room sipping at the iced tea and munching at the gingerbread cookies that Martha Macomber had brought in on a tray. They discussed the weather, the state of business, and the national political situation. Now Carl Macomber spoke up.

"I called you together about this business of the temple down in the Chilton area. It's got me worried. I was in the Ship's Cabin the other night and heard some talk down there that I didn't like. I was sitting in one of the booths, so I wasn't seen, but there were the usual loafers that you find around there, nursing a beer and talking to hear themselves, mostly. They were saying that this rabbi must have done it, and that nothing was being done because the police were being paid off by the Jews;

that Hugh Lanigan and the rabbi were great friends and were always at each other's houses."

"Was it Buzz Applebury who was doing most of the talking?" asked George Collins, an expansive, smiling man. "I had him out to the house a couple of days ago to give me a figure on painting the trim and he was talking that way. Of course, I laughed at him and called him a damn fool."

"It was Buzz Applebury," admitted Macomber, "but there were three or four others there and they seemed to be in pretty general agreement."

"Is that what's troubling you, Carl?" asked Heber Nute. He was a fidgety, irascible man who always appeared to be angry about something. The skin on his bald head seemed stretched tight and a large vein quivered with his annoyance. "Goddam, you can't pay any attention to that kind of character." He sounded indignant that he should have been called to discuss so unimportant a matter.

"You're wrong, Heber, this wasn't just one crank like Applebury. The others seemed to think it was reasonable. This kind of talk has been going around, and it can be dangerous."

"I don't see that you can do very much about it, Carl," observed Collins judiciously, "short of just telling him he's a damn fool the way I did."

"Doesn't seem to have done any good," observed Nute sourly. "Something else is bothering you, Carl. You're not one to get worked up by the likes of Applebury. What is it?"

"It's not just Applebury. I've had remarks passed by other people, customers in my store. I don't like it. I've heard it all along, ever since the case broke. It quieted down a little when they picked up Bronstein but it's got worse ever since he's been released. The general tone is that if it isn't Bronstein, then it has to be the rabbi, and that the case against him is not being prosecuted because he and Hugh Lanigan are friends."

"Hugh is all cop," asserted Nute. "He'd arrest his own son if he were guilty."

"Wasn't it the rabbi who got Bronstein off?" asked Collins.

"That's right, but people don't know that."

"Well, as soon as they find the real killer, it'll all quiet down," said Collins.

"How do you know it won't be the rabbi?" demanded Nute.

"For that matter, how do we know they'll find the killer?" asked Macomber. "An awful lot of cases of this type don't ever get solved. And in the meantime, a lot of damage can be done."

"What kind of damage?" asked Collins.

"A lot of nastiness can be stirred up. Jews tend to be sensitive and edgy, and this is their rabbi."

"That's just too damn bad," said Nute, "but I don't see that we have to use kid gloves just because they're sensitive."

"There are over three hundred Jewish families in Barnard's Crossing," said Macomber. "Since most of them live in the Chilton area, you can figure present market value on their houses at around twenty thousand dollars apiece. Many didn't pay that, but that's what they're worth in today's market on average. Our assessments run fifty percent of market evaluation. That's three hundred times ten thousand, which is three million dollars. Taxes on three million dollars is a lot of taxes."

"Well, if the Jews should move out, then Christians would move in," said Nute. "That wouldn't bother me."

"You don't cotton to Jews, do you, Heber?" asked Macomber.

"No, I can't say that I do."

"How about Catholics and colored people?"

"Can't say as I'm overpartial to them either."

"How about Yankees?" asked Collins with a grin.

"He don't care for them either," said Macomber, also grinning. "That's because he's one himself. We Yankees don't like anybody, including each other, but we tolerate everybody."

Even Heber chuckled.

"Well," Macomber went on, "that's why I asked you to come tonight. I was thinking about Barnard's Crossing and what a change there's been in the last fifteen or twenty years. Our schools today are as good as any in the state. We've got a library that's supposed to be one

172

of the best in towns of this size. We've built a new hospital. We've built miles of sewers and paved miles of streets. It's not only a bigger town than it was fifteen years ago—it's a better town. And it was these Chilton people that did it—Jews *and* Christians. Don't kid yourself. These people in the Chilton area, the Christians I'm talking about now, they're not like us here in Old Town. They're a lot more like their Jewish neighbors. They're young executives and scientists and engineers and professional people generally. They're all college graduates and their wives are college people, and they expect their kids to go to college. And you know what brought them—"

"What brought them," said Nute flatly, "is being half an hour from Boston and near the ocean for the summer."

"There are other towns that are on the ocean, and none of them have done half the things we've done and every one has a higher tax rate," said Macomber quietly. "No, it's something else, maybe the spirit that Jean Pierre Bérnard, that old reprobate, brought with him and left for us. When they were hunting witches in Salem, several of them came here and we hid them out. We've never had a witch-hunt here and I don't want one now."

"Something has happened," said Collins, "something definite that's bothering you, and I don't think it's Buzz Applebury shooting off his mouth, or remarks by your customers either. I never knew you to take any sass from customers. Now what is it, Carl?"

Macomber nodded. "There've been telephone calls, crank calls, sometimes late at night. Becker who has the Lincoln-Ford agency was in to see me about making a bid on the new police cruising car. That's what he said he came for, but during the conversation he managed to mention that the president of their temple, Wasserman, and Abe Casson—you know him—they've been getting calls. I spoke to Hugh about it and he said he hadn't heard, but he wouldn't be a bit surprised if the rabbi wasn't getting a lot of them too."

"There's nothing we can do about that, Carl," said Nute.

'I'm not so sure. If we could give everybody in town the idea that we, the Selectmen, were dead set against this kind of thing, it might help. And since most of it seems to be centered on the rabbi—although if you ask me he's just a handy excuse so Buzz Applebury can make himself a big shot—I was thinking we might use this nonsense the Chamber of Commerce instituted two or three years back, the business of blessing the fleet at the beginning of Race Week, to show we don't approve of what's going on. Now Monsignor O'Brien did it one year and Dr. Skinner did it one year—''

"Pastor Mueller did it last year," said Collins.

"All right, that's two Protestants and one Catholic. Suppose we announce that Rabbi Small is going to do it this year.''

"Dammit, Carl, you can't do that. The Jews don't even have a boat club. The Argonauts have a lot of Catholic members and that's why they asked Monsignor O'Brien. As for the Northern and the Atlantic, they don't have any Catholic members, much less Jews. They wouldn't stand for it. They even kicked about having the monsignor.''

"The town does a lot for the yacht clubs," said Macomber, "and if they were told that the Selectmen were unanimous about this, they'd damn well have to stand for it.''

"But dammit," said Nute, "you can't ask the yacht clubs to let a Jew rabbi bless their boats, no more than you could ask them to let him christen one of their kids.''

"Why not? Who blessed them before the Chamber of Commerce dreamed this up?''

"Nobody.''

"Then the boats don't require any blessing. And I haven't noticed that they've been making any faster time since we started blessing them. So the worst anyone could say was that the rabbi's blessing wouldn't do any good. I don't think it would either, not any more than the pastor's or the monsignor's. But I don't suppose anyone would argue that it would hurt.''

"All right, all right," said Nute. "What do you want us to do?''

"Not a damn thing, Heber. I'll go see the rabbi and

extend the invitation. Just back me up if we run into trouble with the rest of the Board.''

Joe Serafino stood at the entrance to the dining room and checked the house. "Good business, Lennie," he remarked.

"Yeah, it's a nice crowd." Then without moving his lips the headwaiter added, "Note the fuzz—third table from the window."

"How do you know?"

"I can smell a cop, I know that one anyway. He's a state detective."

"Did he speak to you?"

Leonard shrugged his shoulders. "They've been around you know, ever since that business with the girl. But this is the first time one of them came in and ordered a drink."

"Who's the woman with him?"

"Must be his wife."

"So maybe he wants a little relaxation." Suddenly he stiffened. "What's the kid doing here, that Stella?"

"Oh, I meant to tell you. She wanted to see you. I told her I'd let her know when you came in."

"What's she want?"

"I suppose she wants to talk to you about a regular job. I can give her the brush-off, if you like. Tell her you're too busy to see her tonight and that you'll call her."

"Why don't you do that. No, hold it. I'll talk to her."

He left the doorway and began to meander among the tables, stopping every now and then to greet an old customer. Unhurriedly, without looking in her direction, he maneuvered to the table where she was sitting. He said, "What's the score, kid? You come to ask me about a job, you don't sit at a table."

"Mr. Leonard said I should. He said it would look better than waiting in the foyer."

"All right, what do you want?"

"I've got to speak to you—in private."

He thought he detected a threatening note in her voice, so he said, "All right. Where's your coat?"

"In the checkroom."

"Get your coat. Do you know where my car is?"

"In the same place you always keep it?"

"Yeah. You go there and wait for me. I'll follow along."

He continued his rounds of the tables until he reached the kitchen door. He drifted on through and a minute later was hurrying through the parking lot.

Easing in behind the wheel he said, "All right, what's on your mind? I haven't got much time."

"The police came to see me this morning, Mr. Serafino."

"What you tell them?" he said quickly. Then he realized his mistake and, almost casually, asked what they wanted.

"I don't know. I wasn't home. The woman I live with, they spoke to her. They left a name and a phone number I was supposed to call, but I told her if they should call back, to say I hadn't been home all day. I wanted to talk to you first. I'm scared."

"What are you scared about? You don't know what they want you for."

In the darkness he could see her nodding her head. "I got an idea, because they asked her if she knew what time I got home, you know, that night."

He shrugged his shoulders in an elaborate gesture of unconcern. "You were working here that night, so they got to question you. They questioned everybody in the place. Just routine. If they come back again, tell them the truth. You were afraid to go home alone that late at night, it being your first time here, so I drove you home and left you off about a quarter-past one."

"Oh, no, it was earlier, Mr. Serafino."

"Yeah? One o'clock?"

"I looked at the clock when I came in, Mr. Serafino. It was only half-past twelve."

Now he was angry—angry and a little frightened. "You trying to pull something, sister? You trying to put me in the middle of a murder rap?"

"I'm not trying to do anything, Mr. Serafino," she said stubbornly. "I know it was half-past twelve when you dropped me off at my house, a little earlier even, because it was half-past when I got in. I'm not very good at lying, Mr. Serafino, so I thought maybe if I were to go to New York—I got a married sister there—and try to get a job, like in a show, if this was just a routine checkup like you say, they might not bother with me if I wasn't around."

"Well, you got a point there."

"I'd need a little expense money, Mr. Serafino. There'd be my fare, and even if I could live with my sister—and I think maybe it would be better if I didn't, at least at first—I'd still have to pay her board and room rent."

"What'd you have in mind?"

"If I got a job right away, it wouldn't have to be so much, but I ought to have maybe five hundred dollars to be safe."

"A shakedown, eh?" He leaned toward her. "Listen here. You know I had nothing to do with that girl."

"I don't know what to think, Mr. Serafino."

"Yes, you do." He waited for her to speak, but she remained silent. He changed his tone. "This business of going to New York—that's no good. If you were to disappear, the cops would get suspicious right away. And they'd find you, believe me. And five hundred bucks—forget about it. I don't have that kind of money." He drew out his wallet and took out five ten-dollar bills. "I don't mind giving you a stake. And if you need it, you can count on a ten-spot now and then—but nothing big, you understand. And if you behave yourself, I can maybe work you in on a regular job at my club. But that's all. And when the cops ask you what time you got in that night, you'll say you don't remember, but it was late, probably after one. Don't worry about not being a good liar. The cops will expect you to be flustered."

She was shaking her head.

"What's the matter?"

In the dim glow from the club's electric sign he saw a smug little smile on her face.

"If you didn't have anything to do with it, Mr. Serafino, I don't figure you'd give me anything. And if you did, then what you're offering is not enough."

"Look, I had nothing to do with that girl. Get that through your head. Why am I doing this? I'll tell you. Any guy who operates a nightclub, he's fair game for the

177

police. They can raise hell with him, see? If they start bearing down on me, my business goes to pot. That Bronstein guy that they picked up and then let go, he sells cars. So if he finds it hurt his business, he drops his prices or gives better trade-ins for a little while, and that's all. But if the same thing happened to me, I'd have to close up for good. And I'm a married man with a couple of kids. So it's worth a few bucks to me to avoid trouble. But that's all.''

She shook her head.

He sat very still, his fingers drumming lightly on the steering wheel. Then he turned away from her, as if talking to someone else. ''In this business, you run up against all kinds of characters. You need like a kind of insurance, if you're to have any peace of mind. A character starts pushing you, so you try to make a deal. If you can't you get in touch with your—uh—insurance agent. You'd be surprised what kind of service you can get for five hundred bucks. Now where the job's a nice-looking girl like you, there are agents would give me a special rate—maybe not even charge me at all. Some of those guys like to play, especially it's a nice-looking young girl. They do it for kicks.'' He glanced at her from the corner of his eye and knew he was getting through to her. ''Like I said, I want to be friendly. I don't mind helping a friend out now and then. A friend needs a job bad, I can usually arrange it. A friend needs a few bucks, say for a new outfit, I can be touched.''

He held out the money again.

This time she took it.

25

MACOMBER HAD PHONED AHEAD TO MAKE SURE THE RABBI would be in when he arrived.

"Macomber? Do we know a Macomber?" the rabbi asked when Miriam told him about the call.

"He said it was something about town business."

"Do you suppose it's the Selectman? Macomber is the name of the chairman, I believe."

"Why don't you ask him when he gets here?" she said shortly. And then added, as if she realized she had been abrupt, "He said seven o'clock."

The rabbi looked at his wife questioningly but said nothing. She had been moody for several days now, but he did not like to question her.

The rabbi recognized Macomber immediately and started to lead him into his study, assuming he had come on some matter concerning the temple or the Jewish community. But he seemed content to remain in the living room.

"I won't be but a minute, rabbi. I stopped by to ask if you would care to take part in the opening ceremonies of Boat Race Week."

"What sort of part?" asked the rabbi.

"Well, in the last few years we've made quite a thing

179

of it. We get boats from all over, you know, from all the yacht clubs along the North Shore, and quite a few from the South Shore and even further. Before the first race, we have a ceremony on the judge's dock—a band concert, flag-raising and finally the blessing of the fleet. Last couple of years we've had Protestant ministers and before that we've had a Catholic priest. So this year, we thought it would be only fair to have a rabbi, now that we have one in town."

"I'm not sure just what it is that you want me to bless," said the rabbi. "These are pleasure craft of one sort or another that are coming down here to race. Is there any danger involved?"

"Not really. Of course, you can always get hit by a spar when coming about and get thrown into the water, but that doesn't happen very often."

The rabbi was puzzled and uncertain. "Then you want me to pray for victory?"

"Well, naturally we'd like our folks to win, but we're not competing as a town, if that's what you mean."

"Then I'm not quite sure that I understand. You mean that you just want the boats themselves blessed?"

"That's the idea, rabbi. Your job would be to bless the boats, not only ours, but all those that are in the harbor at the time."

"I don't know," said the rabbi doubtfully. "I haven't had much experience in that sort of thing. You see, our prayers are rarely petitionary. We don't so much ask for things that we don't have as give thanks for what we have received."

"I don't understand."

The rabbi smiled. "It's something like this. You Christians say, 'Our Father who art in Heaven, give us this day our daily bread.' Our comparable prayer is, 'Blessed art Thou, O Lord, who bringest forth bread from the earth.' That's rather over-simplified, but in general our prayers tend to be prayers of thanksgiving for what has been given to us. Of course, I could offer thanks for the boats which provide us with the pleasures of sailing. It's a little farfetched; I'd have to think about it. I'm not really in the blessing business, you know."

Macomber laughed. "That's a curious way of putting

it. I don't suppose Monsignor O'Brien who did it a couple of years ago, or Dr. Skinner who took a turn at it one year, think of themselves as being in the blessing business either. But they did it."

"It's at least more appropriate to their respective professions than it is to mine."

"Aren't you all in the same profession?"

"Oh no, we stem from different traditions, all three of us. Monsignor O'Brien is a priest in the tradition of the priests of the Bible, the sons of Aaron. He has certain powers, magical powers, that he exercises in the celebration of the Mass, for example, where the bread and wine are magically changed to the body and blood of Christ. Dr. Skinner as a Protestant minister is in the tradition of the prophets. He has received a call to preach the word of God. I, a rabbi, am essentially a secular figure, having neither the *mana* of the priest nor the 'call' of the minister. If anything, I suppose we come closest to the judges of the Bible."

"Well," said Macomber slowly, "I think I see what you mean, but nobody really—What I mean to say is that we're primarily interested in the ceremony."

"Were you about to say nobody listens to the prayer anyway?"

Macomber laughed shortly. "I'm afraid, rabbi, that I was going to say just that. And now I've offended you."

"Not at all. As a rabbi I am just as aware that people do not listen to my prayers as you are that they don't listen to your most serious arguments. I am not concerned with whether those standing on the dock will be in a mood of proper devotion so much as whether the purpose of the prayer might not be frivolous."

Macomber seemed disappointed.

"Why are you so anxious to have my husband give the prayer?" asked Miriam.

Macomber glanced from one to the other and saw in her even look and in the determined set of her chin that it was futile to temporize. He decided to gamble on the truth.

"It's the bad reaction to this unfortunate business at the temple. Especially the last few days, there's been talk—not nice talk. We've never had anything of this sort and we don't like it. We had the idea it might help matters if we could announce that the Board of Selectmen had invited you to bless the fleet. I agree with you, it's pretty silly—a brainstorm the Chamber of Commerce dreamed up a few years back. Oh, it's done in some Catholic countries in the small fishing villages, but there ships are serious business and their success affects the whole economy. And there's considerable danger, too. It's even reasonable in Gloucester, where the big fleets sail from. Here it's just meaningless ceremony, but as far as you're concerned, rabbi, it will serve to underscore the fact that the Selectmen—and therefore the responsible people in town—will have no part of these shameful acts."

"That's very kind of you, Mr. Macomber," the rabbi said, "but aren't you perhaps exaggerating the situation?"

"No, believe me. You personally may not have suffered any annoyance or embarrassment, or if you have you may have shrugged it off as the work of a crackpot or two that will stop when the real culprit is caught. But this kind of case is the hardest to solve and frequently doesn't get solved at all. In the meantime, some very decent people can be hurt. I don't say that this scheme will solve the situation, but I'm sure it'll help a little."

"I appreciate what you are trying to do and the spirit that prompts it—"

"Then you agree?"

The rabbi shook his head slowly.

"Why not? Is it against your religion?"

"As a matter of fact, it is. It's specifically mentioned: Thou shalt not take the name of the Lord thy God in vain."

Macomber rose. "I guess there's nothing more to be said but I wish you'd think about it. It's not just you, you understand, it's the whole Jewish community."

When he left, Miriam exclaimed, "Oh David, these are good people."

He nodded but said nothing.

The telephone rang and he picked up the receiver. "Rabbi Small," he said, and then listened. She watched him, alarmed as she saw the color rise in his face. He put the instrument back on its rest and turned to his wife. "Is that the kind of wrong number you've been getting?" he said quietly.

She nodded.

"The same person each time?"

"Sometimes it's a man's voice and sometimes a woman's. It has never seemed like the same voice twice. Several times it has been just a string of obscenities, but most of the time they say terrible things."

"This person, quite a nice voice by the way, wanted to know if human sacrifice was required for our approaching festival—I suppose he was referring to Pesach."

"Oh no!"

"Oh yes."

"It's terrible. This lovely town has such nice people like Hugh Lanigan and Mr. Macomber, and then those people on the phone . . ."

"Crackpots," he said in contemptuous dismiss. "Just a few nasty crackpots."

"It's not only the phone calls, David."

"No? What else?"

"When I go into the stores, the clerks used to be so warm. Now they're polite. And the other customers, those I know, they try to avoid me."

"You're sure you're not imagining it?" But he sounded less certain of himself.

"Quite sure, David. isn't there something you can do?"

"Such as what?"

"I don't know. You're the rabbi; you're supposed to know. Maybe you ought to tell Hugh Lanigan what's been happening. Maybe you ought to consult a lawyer. Maybe you ought to consider Macomber's offer."

He made no answer but returned to the living room. She looked in to find him sitting in his armchair, his eyes staring fixedly at the wall opposite. When she offered to make him some tea, he shook his head with annoyance. Later she ventured to look in again, and he was still in his chair, his eyes staring straight ahead.

"Will you unzip me, please?" she asked.

Without rising and quite automatically, he pulled at the zipper on the back of her dress. He seemed to come to, for he asked, "Why are you taking off your dress?"

183

"Because I'm exhausted and I want to go to bed."

He laughed. "Why, of course. How stupid of me. You can't very well go to bed with your dress on. If you don't mind, I'll stay up a little while longer."

Just then they heard a car drive up and stop at the door. "Someone is coming," he said. "Who could it be at this hour?"

They waited, and after a while the doorbell rang. Miriam, who had quickly zipped herself up, went to answer, but even as she approached there was the sound of a roaring motor and wheels spinning against gravel. She opened the door and looked out. She saw the taillight of a car speeding down the street in the darkness.

Behind her, she heard her husband exclaim, "Oh my God!" She turned and then saw it too: a swastika on the door, the red paint still fresh and dripping like blood.

He put out a tentative forefinger and stared dumbly at the red spot on his finger. All at once Miriam burst into tears.

"I'm sorry, David," she sobbed.

He held her close until he felt she had regained her composure. Then, his voice harsh, he said: "Get me some of that household cleaning stuff and a rag."

She pressed her face against his shoulder. "I'm afraid, David, I'm afraid."

26

ALTHOUGH THE RABBI'S PICTURE HAD BEEN IN THE PAPERS as one of those connected with the case, Mrs. Serafino did not recognize him when he rang her bell.

I am Rabbi Small," he said. "I should like to talk to you for a few minutes."

She was not sure she ought to, and would have liked to ask her husband, but he was still asleep.

"Is it about the case? Because if it is, I don't think I should."

"I came to see her room." There was something so positive and assured in his tone that to refuse seemed almost impertinent.

She hesitated and then said, "I guess it will be all right. It's back here beyond the kitchen," and she led the way.

The telephone rang on their way into the kitchen and she raced over to pick it up at the first ring. She talked for a moment and then hung up. "Excuse me," she said to the rabbi. "We have an extension beside our bed, and I didn't want to wake Joe."

"I understand."

She opened a door from the kitchen and stood aside so he could enter. He looked around the room—at the bed, at the night table beside it, at the bureau, at the small armchair. He went to the night table and read the titles of the few books on its shelf; he glanced at the small plastic radio on top of the table. He studied it for a moment and then turned the knob and waited until he heard a voice announce, "This is Station WSAM, Salem's own station, bringing you music—"

"I don't think you're supposed to touch anything," she said.

He turned it off and smiled apologetically. "She play it much?"

"All the time—this crazy rock and roll music."

The door of the closet stood open. He asked her permission and then looked inside. Mrs. Serafino herself opened the door to the bathroom.

"Thank you," he said. "I've seen enough."

She led the way back to the living room. "Did you find anything special?"

"I didn't expect to. I just wanted to get some idea about the girl. Tell me, was she pretty?"

"She was no beauty, for all the newspapers kept calling her 'an attractive blonde.' I guess they call any girl that. She was sort of attractive in a corn-fed farm-girl sort of way, you know, thick waist, thick legs and ankles—oh, I'm sorry."

"It's all right, Mrs. Serafino," he reassured her, "I know about ankles and legs. Tell me, did she seem happy?"

"I guess so."

"And yet I understood she had no friends."

"Well, she and this Celia who works for the Hoskins a couple of houses down sometimes went to a movie together."

"Any men friends, or wouldn't you have known?"

"I think she would have told me if she had a date. You know how it is, two women in a house together, they talk. But I'm sure there were no men friends. When she went to a movie Thursday nights, she'd either go alone or with Celia. Yet in the papers it said she was pregnant, so I guess she must have known at least one man."

186

"That Thursday, was there anything unusual about her behavior?"

"No, it was about like any other Thursday. I was busy, so she took care of the children's lunch, but she left right after. Usually she would go out before."

"But it was not unusual for her to leave when she did?"

"I wouldn't say so."

"Well thank you, Mrs. Serafino, you have been very kind."

She went to the door with him and watched him walk down the path. Then she called after him, "Rabbi Small—there's Celia now if you want to talk to her, the girl with the two children." She watched him hasten down the street and accost the girl.

Rabbi Small spoke to Celia for a few minutes and then walked to the corner of the street and glanced at the mailbox. He got into his car and drove to Salem, where he spent some time before driving back home.

Mr. Serafino got up shortly after noon. He washed, rubbed his hand against his blue-black beard stubble and decided not to shave until evening, and went down to the kitchen. Outside in the backyard he saw his wife playing with the children and he waved. She came in to serve him his breakfast and he sat at the kitchen table reading the comics in the morning newspaper while she puttered at the stove.

Not until he finished breakfast did a word pass between them. Then she said, "I'll bet you'll never guess who was here this morning."

He made no reply.

"It was that Rabbi Small from the Jewish temple," she went on. "You know, the one whose car they found the bag in."

"What'd he want?"

"He wanted to ask me about the girl."

"He's got a nerve. You didn't say anything?"

"I talked to him. Why not?"

He looked at her in astonishment. "Because he's a party to the case and what you know is evidence, that's why not."

"But he seemed like such a nice sort of young man, not like what you'd expect a rabbi to be. I mean, he didn't have a beard or anything."

"None of them do these days. Don't you remember the Golds' wedding we went to last year. That rabbi didn't have a beard either."

"He wasn't even like that, you know, dignified. He was just an ordinary young fellow, like he might be an insurance salesman or a car salesman, but not a fast-talker, just nice and polite. He wanted to see the girl's room."

"And you showed it to him?"

"Sure I did."

"The police told you to keep the door shut. How do you know he wasn't planning to take something or rub out a fingerprint or even leave something behind?"

"Because I was with him all the time. He only stayed a couple of seconds altogether."

"Well, I'll tell you what I'm going to do. I'm going to call the police and report it." He rose.

"But why?"

"Because this is a murder case, and what's in that room is evidence, and he's a party to the case, and he might have been tampering with the evidence. And hereafter, don't you go talking about this case to anybody, you understand?"

"All right."

"Anybody, get it?"

"All right."

"I don't want you should say one single, solitary word, you understand."

"All right, all right. What are you so excited for? You're all red in the face."

"A guy has a right to have some peace and quiet in his own house," he raged.

She smiled at him. "You're just edgy, Joe. C'mon, sit down, baby, and let me get you another cup of coffee."

He sat down and ducked behind his newspaper. She got a fresh cup and saucer and poured his coffee. She was puzzled and uncertain and worried.

27

THE RABBI WAS NOT ALTOGETHER SURPRISED WHEN HUGH Lanigan dropped in that evening.

"I understand you went calling on the Serafinos this morning," he said.

The young man reddened and nodded.

"You were sleuthing, weren't you, rabbi?" Lanigan's lips twitched in an effort to be stern, although he obviously thought the situation amusing. "Don't do it, rabbi. You could muddy the trail, and Lord knows it's obscure enough as it is. I might also mention that it could excite suspicion. Mr. Serafino, who called to tell us about it, thought you might have come there to remove something, presumably something incriminating, from the girl's room."

"I had no idea," he said contritely. "I'm sorry." He hesitated, and then went on timidly, "I had an idea I wanted to check."

Lanigan shot him a quick glance. "Yes?"

The rabbi nodded and went on hurriedly, "In any sequence of events there's a beginning and a middle and an end. The last time we discussed this case, I'm afraid we started at the end, with the handbag. I suggest you would get further if you started at the beginning."

"And what do you call the beginning? The girl's getting pregnant?"

"That could be the beginning, but we have no real certainty that was connected with the girl's death."

"Then where would you start?"

"If I were conducting the investigation," said the rabbi, "I would first want to know why she left the house after Bronstein brought her home."

Lanigan considered the suggestion and then shrugged his shoulders. "She could have left for any number of reasons, to mail a letter perhaps."

"Then why take off her dress?"

"It was raining at the time," Lanigan observed. "Maybe she didn't want to get the dress wet."

"Then she would simply have slipped on a coat or raincoat—as she did. Besides, mail is not collected until nine-thirty the next morning. I looked at the box."

"All right, then she didn't go out to mail a letter. Maybe she just wanted to take a short walk, to get some air."

"In the rain? After she had been out all afternoon and evening? Besides, the same objection holds—why would she take off her dress? That's really the basic question: why did she take off her dress?"

"All right, why did she?"

"Why, to go to bed," announced the rabbi.

Lanigan stared at the triumphant look on his face. Finally he said, "I don't get it. What are you driving at?"

The rabbi could not help showing some impatience. "The girl comes home from a night out. It's late and she has to get up early the next morning. So she starts to prepare for bed. She takes off her dress and hangs it up carefully in the closet. Normally she would have gone on to take off the rest of the things, but something interrupted her in the process. I suggest it could only have been a message of some sort."

"You mean she got a telephone call?"

Rabbi Small shook his head. "She couldn't have because there is an extension upstairs and Mrs. Serafino would have heard the phone ring."

"Then how?"

"The radio. According to Mrs. Serafino she had it on all the time. With girls of that age, turning on the radio is a conditioned reflex. As automatic as breathing. I suggest she turned it on as soon as she came in."

"All right, so she turned on the radio. What sort of message could she have received?"

"There's a news round-up from WSAM, the Salem station, at 12:35. The last few minutes are devoted to local news."

"And you think she heard a bit of local news that sent her scurrying out into the rain? Why?"

"Because she had to meet someone."

"At that hour? How could she know where to meet this someone. I know that program—it doesn't run personals. And if she was meeting someone, why didn't she put on a dress first? Really, rabbi—"

"She didn't have time to put on a dress because she had to get there by one o'clock," said the rabbi quietly. "And she knew he would be there because that was the time he was supposed to ring in at the police box."

Lanigan stared at him. "You mean—Bill Norman?"

The rabbi nodded.

"But that's impossible. He just became engaged to Bud Ramsay's girl. I went to the engagement party. It was that very night. I was one of the guests of honor."

"Yes, I know. That was the announcement over the radio. I called the station today and checked. Think about it for a minute, and keep in mind the fact that the girl was pregnant. According to all those who knew her, the only time she was ever in the company of men—socially, that is—was her one excursion to Old Town, the Policemen's Ball. I suggest she met Norman there."

"You're not suggesting the keel for her little ship was laid at the Policemen's Ball?"

"Hardly. That was back in February. But that's where she first made Norman's acquaintance. I'm not sure how it was renewed, but I can imagine. Like most laymen, I know that the patrolman on his beat is required to call in at regular intervals. I had always assumed that like a night watchman in a factory, the time between calls depended on the length of time it took him to walk from one box to the next."

"Well, not exactly," Lanigan began. "He's given a certain leeway."

"So I discovered some weeks ago when I was called on to settle a dispute between two members of our congregation. One of them had to get into a house late at night without a key, and the cab driver rounded up the patrolman on duty who made it a practice to stop off nearby for an unofficial coffee break."

"It's an eight-hour tour of duty. You can't expect a man to be on his feet all that time without a rest," said Lanigan defensively. "And in the winter a man has to warm up every now and then."

"Of course," the rabbi agreed, "and thinking it over, I realized that it was only common sense to allow him considerable leeway, if only because of the investigating he might have to do along the way. I spoke to Officer Johnson, who patrols this same beat during the day, and he explained that the night patrolman usually makes his own arrangements. On this route, for example, he stops with the night watchman for a while at the Gordon block. Then there is the milk plant, and when Stanley was staying overnight at the temple that was another stop. Now here is the Serafino house, and except for the children who are asleep upstairs Elspeth is all alone until two o'clock or later every morning. Along comes a dashing young policeman, a bachelor moreover, who has to ring in a box on the corner of Maple and Vine streets at one o'clock and whose beat then takes him down Vine Street right near the Serafino house. So on cold, bitter nights, what better arrangement than to drop in on the girl for a hot cup of coffee and a pleasant chat for half an hour before going out into the night again."

"But how about Thursdays? Wouldn't she expect him to take her out on her night off?"

"Why should he? She was seeing him every other night in the week. And he was on night duty, so he needed his sleep during the day. I imagine she loved him and presumed that he loved her. She probably expected to marry him. There is nothing to indicate she was a loose girl. On the contrary, that's probably why she did not go out with other men and refused to double-date with Celia. She considered herself engaged."

"It's ingenious," admitted Lanigan, "but it's all conjectural."

"Granted, but it all adds up. And it enables us to reconstruct the events of that fatal Thursday in the only way that makes sense. She suspects she's pregnant, so she goes to an obstetrician on her day off. She gets dressed up nicely, not forgetting to wear a wedding ring. Was it her mother's, or did she buy it in the fond hope that she would be wearing it legitimately shortly? At the doctor's office, she gives her name as Mrs. Elizabeth Brown, not because of Bronstein whom she hadn't met as yet but because it is a common name like Smith and because it is natural to retain the same initials. She is examined and the doctor tells her she is pregnant.

"Now Bronstein said that when he first saw her in the restaurant, she kept glancing at the clock as if she were waiting for someone. I imagine you have since verified with the waitresses that she didn't order when she first came into the restaurant. My guess is that since they normally didn't see each other on Thursdays, she had phoned her lover and made a special appointment with him."

"The doctor's secretary said she asked if there was a pay station in the building," Lanigan remarked.

The rabbi nodded. "Norman must have agreed, or at least said he would try to make it, so she went to the Surfside to wait."

"Yet she went out with Bronstein."

"She probably felt hurt when he didn't show up—hurt and perhaps apprehensive. Bronstein said that he went over only when he decided she had been, er—stood up, and then all he did was ask her to join him because he did not like to eat alone. He was a much older man and she probably saw no danger in it. After all, she was in a restaurant, a public place. During the course of the meal, she evidently concluded that he was a decent sort, so she consented to spend the evening with him. She probably wanted company badly—she must have been feeling pretty blue at the time. He brought her home and she got ready for bed. She had taken off her dress when she heard the announcement of Norman's engagement."

"So knowing that Norman was due to ring in at Maple

193

and Vine at one o'clock and it was then, say, five of, she had to dash. She threw on her coat and because it was raining and she had several blocks to go, her raincoat over that, and went to meet him. Is that it, rabbi?"

"I would say so."

"And then what do you think happened?"

"Well, it was raining, and quite hard. He had seen my car parked outside the temple and I suppose he suggested they get in and talk it over. They got in the back seat and he offered her a cigarette. They talked for a while. Perhaps they quarreled. Perhaps she threatened to go to his fiancée. So he seized the chain she was wearing and twisted. He could not leave the body in the car, of course, since I suppose he was expected to give at least a cursory inspection to any vehicle parked outside all night. If the body had been found in the car, he'd have had some explaining to do. So he carried it out to the grass plot and hid it behind the wall. The handbag had slid to the floor and he just didn't notice it."

"Of course you realize, rabbi, that we don't have an iota of proof for any of this."

The rabbi nodded.

"But it certainly does all hang together," Lanigan went on reflectively. "If she had gone to the Ramsays with her story, that would have ended his engagement to Alice. I know the Ramsays. Decent people—but proud. I also thought I knew him." He raised an inquisitive eyebrow at the rabbi. "You had this all figured out and then went to the Serafinos' to check your theory?"

"Not really. I had a vague notion, but it was not until I had seen the radio in the girl's room that the explanation began to form. Of course, I had an advantage over you because I had reason to be suspicious of Officer Norman from the beginning."

"What do you mean?"

"He denied that he saw me, but I knew that he had. What reason could he have? Since he did not know me, it could not be a personal dislike. If he had admitted seeing me, it would not have helped his position in any way—only mine. It would have established the fact that I had already left the temple well before the murder had been committed. But if he were guilty or in some way involved, wouldn't it be to his advantage to have suspicion point at someone else?"

"Why didn't you tell me this before, rabbi?"

"Because it was only a suspicion, and besides, it is not easy for a rabbi to point a finger at a man and say he is a murderer."

Lanigan was silent.

"Of course we still have no real proof," the rabbi ventured.

"I'm not worried about getting it."

"What do you propose to do?"

"Well, at the moment," said Lanigan, "I'm not sure whether to ask Norman what Elspeth Bleech said to him on the phone Thursday afternoon, or why he didn't keep his appointment with her at the Surfside Restaurant. In the meantime, I'll arrange for that girl Celia to have a look at him. She said Elspeth was with one man most of the evening at the Policemen's Ball. If your theory's right, I figure that would be Norman. And we'll question the Simpsons who live across the street from the Serafinos. If he saw her as often as you think he did, they may have noticed him going in there late at night." His lips relaxed in a tight little smile. "When we know what we're looking for, rabbi, we don't have too much trouble finding it."

28

THE BOARD MEETING WAS UNUSUAL IN THAT THE RABBI WAS
present. When Jacob Wasserman had come to him and
asked if he would be willing to sit with the board at their
regular meeting, he was pleased and grateful.

"You don't have to, you know. I mean, we won't
hold it against you if you don't come to a meeting, or to
any of them for that matter. I just want you to know that
any time you choose to come, we'll be happy to have
you."

And now he was present at his first meeting. He
listened carefully to the secretary read the minutes of
the previous meeting. He was most attentive during the
reports of the chairmen of various committees. The principal piece of Old Business was a motion to floodlight
the parking lot at night.

The original motion had been made by Al Becker and
he now rose to speak. "I've done a little checking around.
We've got this electrical contractor that does a lot of
work for us and I had him come out and look the place
over and give us a very rough figure as to the cost.
According to him, we can do it in one of two ways.
Either put up three towers, which would come to about
twelve hundred apiece, or we could put up six special

floodlights mounted on the temple itself. Mounting them would be cheaper, but it would spoil the outline of the building. We could get those for five hundred apiece, so it's three thousand against thirty-six hundred. Then we'd have to have a clock arrangement to turn the lights on and off automatically. That wouldn't cost much, but we'd have to figure in the cost of electricity. All told, the job could be done for five thousand bucks at the outside.''

Becker was nettled at the groan from those around the table. "I know it's a lot of money, but this is necessary. I'm glad our rabbi is here today because no one knows better than he how important it is to have our parking lot lit up at night.''

"But think what it will cost us year after year, Al. You can't put sixty-watt bulbs in those babies. In the winter, that can be about fourteen hours.''

"Would you rather have the place become a lovers' lane, or maybe have another little business like the one we had?'' Becker shot back.

"In the summer, those lights will attract a zillion mosquitoes.''

"So—they'll be up around near the light, won't they? If anything, it will keep the grounds free of them.''

"That's not the way it works up at the driving range. When they have those lights on, the mosquitoes are all over the place.''

"And how do you think the people that live nearby are going to like having a place the size of the parking lot lit up all night?''

The rabbi murmured something.

"What is it, rabbi?'' Mr. Wasserman asked. "Did you want to say something on this matter?''

"I was just thinking,'' said the rabbi diffidently, "there's only one car entrance to the parking lot. Why can't you just put up a gate?''

There was sudden silence. Then they all started to explain it to each other.

"Sure, it's asphalt so nobody would come there except in a car.''

"There are bushes and shrubs all around the front. All we'd have to block off is the driveway.''

"Stanley could close it every night and open it first thing in the morning."

"Even if Stanley weren't around some night and a committee wanted to hold a meeting, so they could park their cars in the street."

As suddenly as they had begun, they stopped and looked at their young rabbi with respect and admiration.

The rabbi was at home, a large volume on the desk in front of him, when his wife came to the door of the study. "Chief Lanigan is here, dear."

The rabbi started to rise, but Lanigan said, "Don't get up, rabbi." Then he noticed the volume on the desk. "Am I interrupting?"

"Not at all."

"Nothing special," Lanigan went on. "Ever since we solved the case I've missed our little chats. But I was in the neighborhood, so out of habit I thought I'd drop in and say hello."

The rabbi smiled his pleasure.

"I just came up against a little bit of pedantry that might amuse you," Lanigan said. "You know, every two weeks I have to submit the salary schedule for the department to the town comptroller for audit and approval. I list the regular hours worked by each man, overtime if any, special assignments, and then total it up for each man. You understand?"

The rabbi nodded.

"Well, I had the whole thing turned back to me" —Lanigan could not keep the exasperation from showing in his voice—"because Patrolman Norman was included for his full tour of duty. The comptroller claimed he should have been docked for all the time after he killed the girl because, as a criminal, he was no longer entitled to be on the police payroll. How do you like that? I don't know whether to fight him on it, or just drop the item and forget about it."

The rabbi pursed his lips and then glanced at the big book on his desk. He smiled. "Shall we see what the Talmud says?"

ABOUT THE AUTHOR

Harry Kemelman is the author of the eight best-selling *Rabbi* novels. He lives in the Boston area.

Scholar, Rabbi... and Detective!

The Inimitable Rabbi David Small books

by

Harry Kemelman

11   Allow at least 4 weeks for delivery.   TAF-72